# "Trinity, whatever it is, just tell me."

"Michael's aunt and uncle's court case has nothing to do with the businesses."

"How so?" Rhett asked.

"Those might help them. But that's not why they want the inheritance."

She turned to a gorgeous portrait of a house. Despite the grandeur of the building, Rhett felt the promise of protection within its walls. A small name plate confirmed this was Maison de Jardin.

"Whoever gains control of Michael's inheritance doesn't just gain his place on the board of the businesses. They gain control over the charity, with nothing to mitigate their decisions."

"There's no board for the charity?"

Trinity s[...]hecks and balanc[...] de Jardin whatev[...] one to stop them."

"From d[...]

"What they've wanted all along...to sell Maison de Jardin to the highest bidder."

\* \* \*

*Entangled with the Heiress* by Dani Wade
is part of the Louisiana Legacies series.

Dear Reader,

I'll admit that my heroine in *Entangled with the Heiress*, Trinity Hyatt, ends up in a situation that few of us ever would. She marries her best friend and ends up a widow before they can even announce their marriage. She knows all about the challenges in life and feels she owes her friend everything after he rescued her and her mother from an abusive home.

Living with suspicions and dispersions on all sides might make a woman give up, but Trinity is one of the rare few with a purpose. I'm so proud of her for standing up for herself and the abused women in her care. I hope her determination to build a life of meaning despite the abuse she was subjected to as a child inspires you in some way, as it has me.

Please enjoy my new Louisiana Legacies series.

I love to hear from my readers! You can email me at readdaniwade@gmail.com or follow me on Facebook. As always, news about my releases is easiest to find through my author newsletter, which you can sign up for from my website at www.daniwade.com.

Enjoy!

*Dani*

# DANI WADE

—

# ENTANGLED WITH THE HEIRESS

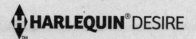

**HARLEQUIN**®DESIRE

ISBN-13: 978-1-335-20887-3

Entangled with the Heiress

**HARLEQUIN**®
www.Harlequin.com

**Printed in U.S.A.**

**Dani Wade** astonished her local librarians as a teenager when she carried home ten books every week—and actually read them all. Now she writes her own characters, who clamor for attention in the midst of the chaos that is her life. Residing in the southern United States with her husband, two kids, two dogs and one grumpy cat, she stays busy until she can closet herself away with her characters once more.

### Books by Dani Wade

### Harlequin Desire

#### Milltown Millionaires

*A Bride's Tangled Vows*
*The Blackstone Heir*
*The Renegade Returns*
*Expecting His Secret Heir*

#### Savannah Sisters

*Taming the Billionaire*
*Son of Scandal*

#### Louisiana Legacies

*Entangled with the Heiress*

Visit her Author Profile page at Harlequin.com, or daniwade.com, for more titles.

You can also find Dani Wade on Facebook, along with other Harlequin Desire authors, at Facebook.com/harlequindesireauthors.

This book is dedicated to my daughter, Nicole, who is finding her purpose and passions in life just like Trinity. I'm proud of the woman you have become, but you'll always be my little curly-headed "baby girl." Go forth and conquer!

# One
_____

Trinity Hyatt walked down the museum hallway, keeping her steps light on the tile floor as if she were a child trying to sneak past her parents. As if the sound of the gala from the west wing wouldn't cover her brief getaway.

She just needed a moment, a moment away from the speculative gazes and prying questions. A moment to breathe...

But then she thought back to the headline she'd seen when she turned on her computer this morning.

Suspicious Marriage Threatens
Local Jobs

_That damn blogger_... Her mother had drilled into her growing up that using profanity was only for the uneducated, but Trinity had found its occasional use more than satisfying as an adult. Since the mental slip was the only form of anger Trinity allowed herself, she hoped her mother forgave her this time.

Didn't the anonymous columnist understand how much words hurt? Not to mention how the photograph that accompanied the story made Trinity relive the moment standing beside Michael's grave as half the country watched and ultimately judged her. Why couldn't her online tormentor see the grief on her face? Why couldn't this person tell her tears were genuine?

Trinity locked away the memories of the painful whispering and curious stares during tonight's charity gala, brought on by today's post. Instead she tried to focus on her momentary solitude in one of her favorite places in New Orleans.

So many memories from the familiar hallways of the ASTRA Museum flitted through her overtaxed mind, bringing a welcome peace. She remembered holding her mother's hand as they walked in the blessed quiet, without worry over someone yelling at them or telling them to leave because they didn't fit in because they were too poor. The museum had been open without cost every Saturday. They'd often made the trip across town on the bus to spend a few hours away from her screaming father, looking at the paintings and sculptures, appreciating the beauty that drew them even though they knew nothing about art.

Later, Michael had wandered these halls with her, filling her mind with stories of the artists and the sometimes harrowing journeys the pieces went through before coming to be displayed in the Southern United States.

They were both gone now, to Trinity's never-ending grief. But she tucked it down inside and locked it away, because Michael had left her with a very important job to do. And she would. She would step back out into the charity event with her head high and represent her best friend and everything he'd worked so hard to build.

But for just a moment, she needed peace and calm to surround her.

A twinge of guilt stole through her as she reflected on her husband…though it was still hard to think of him as such. Ten years her senior, Michael Hyatt had been her friend and mentor of sorts for a long time. Then they'd barely been married a week. She had trouble accepting that he was gone, though the explosive crash of his private helicopter had taken him from her just a little over six weeks ago.

The ache he'd left behind weighed on her day and night.

Coming to a standstill in front of a hundred-year-old painting of a peasant woman holding her infant son, Trinity stared at the muted colors. Her vision blurred, the familiar details disappearing as her brain simply drifted. Even the ache this particular portrait always evoked inside her remained subdued. Children were another part of her life to be mourned, and she didn't want to handle that tonight.

When her eyes felt too full, she let her lids close, ignoring the solitary tear that flowed down her cheek.

"She looks happy... At peace, wouldn't you say? Despite what must be hard life circumstances."

Startled to hear an echo of her own past thoughts on this particular painting, Trinity turned. She hadn't heard anyone approach. But the man now standing beside her took her very breath away.

His dark hair had a touch of premature silver at each temple. The color echoed the cool gray of his irises, which had subtle green striations. His bearing was distinguished enough that he fit into the elegant surroundings of the museum, but he didn't have the soft edges that a lifetime of high living gave many men in this world. Head and shoulders taller than her own average height, he left Trinity feeling dwarfed. He filled out his tux just enough to hint at muscle without too much bulk.

His gaze dropped to her cheek, leaving Trinity uncomfortably aware of the cool air over her moist skin. As casually as she could manage, she wiped the tear away. He didn't mention what he'd seen.

The very look of him mesmerized her even more than the paintings. An embarrassingly long moment drew out before she could force herself to breathe in a long drink of air, then she offered a small nod. "Yes, I've always thought so."

For the briefest instant, a surprised expression crossed his features. She noticed a faint lifting of one dark brow, so quick she wondered if it had even happened.

Trinity stiffened. The question of whether or not he was a reporter hadn't occurred to her, but having seen that same expression on the faces of the people who hounded her day in and day out, she couldn't help but wonder. Had he followed her here on purpose?

Having swallowed the story that she'd been raised in a rural, strictly religious household, most press hounds didn't expect her to speak with a cultured accent or intelligent words. After all, she had to be a money-hungry hick to have come from obscurity to inherit the entire Hyatt fortune. It was the very image that Michael's family had painted of her.

That idea sold more stories, more of the candid pictures they hunted her down for. They didn't want to look for the truth, the *deeper* truth of who she was, of what she'd survived.

But the man's expression disappeared so quickly that Trinity wondered if she was just being paranoid because of her current situation. Now his cool gaze trailed down her sapphire gown, one of the few Michael had personally picked out for her. For once, Trinity wasn't left feeling vulnerable and exposed. Instead a small wave of unexpected heat flowed over her.

"Needed a little breather from the party?" he asked quietly.

Though it was probably a banal piece of small talk, Trinity was shaken at how much it echoed her own thoughts. She tried to brush it off. "These things do tend to get a little stuffy at times."

"I agree. In many ways."

Goodness, that grin reached all the way to the core of her. Something Trinity had never experienced before… and wasn't really comfortable experiencing now.

To her relief, his gaze moved past her to the elaborate

cream-and-gold walls of the rotunda, pausing at each of the twelve specially chosen pieces displayed permanently within this space. "This isn't just peaceful. It's unique. Gorgeous," he said, his voice deepening in a way that sent a tingle down her spine.

What was wrong with her tonight?

"You've never been here before?" she asked to fill the silence.

Part of her was resentful that this man, and the sensations he seemed to be calling to the surface, had interrupted her time in this special space. The other part of her couldn't quell the fascination that kept popping up in unexpected, uninvited ways.

*I'm a widow, dang it. A recent one.*

Unaware of her inner turmoil, the man answered, "No. This is my first time. My first time in New Orleans, actually." He held out a hand. "I'm Rhett Butler. Nice to meet you."

Trinity felt her mouth drop open in a most unladylike way. "Seriously?"

"No," he said, flashing another hundred-watt smile, "actually my name is Rhett Brannon. But when in the South…"

*Stinker.* "That's good. I was beginning to think your parents had a strange sense of humor." Not that his dark good looks and riveting charisma wouldn't allow him to double for Rhett Butler.

Something deep inside warned her not to make nice. The outstretched hand reminded her of a snake she knew was dangerous. It caused a combination of fascination and fear in her suspicious brain. She couldn't risk one misstep in the game Michael had begged her to play.

She stretched her hand out and politely shook. "Thank you. I'm Trinity, Trinity—Hyatt."

Her hesitation was automatic. Even after almost two months, she had a hard time grasping that her last name had changed, that there was now a paramount need to present herself as Michael's wife. He had counted on her. The charity counted on her. She had to do the right thing.

"Trinity, huh?" Rhett said, not showing any recognition of who she was. Was he simply a good actor? Or did he really not know? "That's an interesting name, too."

Definitely. "My mother was highly religious." She let a small smile stretch her lips. "I've always wondered if it was a reminder to me. To never forget the Father, Son and Holy Ghost."

"And have you?"

She was startled enough to answer honestly. "Some days are easier than others."

The rueful grin that stretched his lips fascinated her more than it should have. "I can agree with that," he said.

A small silence fell, bringing with it that uncomfortable sense of awareness of his masculinity and presence. It only eased a little as he motioned for them to stroll farther around the rotunda.

At least she didn't have to look directly into those mesmerizing eyes. But the silence didn't sit well with her. "So what brings you to NOLA?" she asked.

"Business. Some people I'll be working with brought me along tonight."

"Generous of them."

His grunt could have been a confirmation, but she suspected she heard a bit of skepticism behind the sound.

"Are you here with your husband?"

Surprise shot through her, until her quick glance found his gaze resting on the band encircling her ring finger, the tiny cluster of emeralds and diamonds twinkling in the lights from above. "No," she murmured. "I'm a widow."

It still felt weird saying it out loud. It still felt strange to realize she and Michael had been married. For her, it had essentially been a business proposition—with infinite benefits considering the fortune she stood to inherit. And a favor to the man who had been her best friend, even if it had turned out to be the hardest job she'd ever faced.

And she faced it alone, now that Michael was gone.

Rhett cocked his head to the side, an obvious question in his expression.

"My...husband, Michael Hyatt, passed away recently in an accident."

Rhett's nod was slow and sage. "Yes, I believe I heard about that. Helicopter accident, wasn't it? Very sad."

Of course, he would have heard of it. Michael had not just been a lifelong friend and the owner of the charity Trinity had run for him, he'd also been a wildly successful, multimillion-dollar businessman. The question was, what else had he heard?

As if he sensed her subtle withdrawal, Rhett paused to meet her gaze head on. There was nowhere for her to hide. "Please accept my sincere condolences for your loss."

Startled, she felt pinned by both his look and his words. His wasn't one of the trite *I'm sorry*s that preceded the endless questions she wished she never had to answer again.

"Thank you," she said simply.

"You're welcome." A smaller version of his grin appeared, but dang if it wasn't just as charming.

For a moment, Trinity found herself drifting, wishing she wasn't Michael's widow, wasn't the most talked-about person in New Orleans at the moment, and was simply a woman who could respond to that smile without a worry in the world.

But she wasn't. Time ticked inside her head, counting off the seconds until someone realized she was missing from the elite crowd.

"I really should be getting back," she said. Someone had surely noticed she was gone by now. Especially Michael's aunt and uncle. They didn't miss a move that she made.

And neither did the press.

Defeat weighed down on her as she remembered reading today's post and photos on the *NOLA Secrets & Scandals* blog. She'd never have noticed it on her own. Jenny, her secretary, had pointed it out. The hints about a money-hungry widow threatening the livelihoods of countless families gave her an idea of what information the author had hunted down, but not an idea of when the full story would hit… As if Trinity didn't have enough to stress her out.

Didn't anyone understand that she shared the questions—and fears—about how her husband's death and the lawsuit filed against his estate by his aunt and uncle would affect the business's 50,000-person global workforce?

She assured herself time and again that she was carrying out Michael's wishes. But she had to wonder what he'd been thinking to put a global empire and the fate of that many people under the direction of a charity program director like herself. Still, despite her many misgivings, she never let her worries surface in public. There were too many people eager to use them against her.

Though the question haunted her night after night, she was determined to do her very best by all of them… including Michael.

But those worries were nothing compared to the butterflies in her stomach and unfamiliar heat in her core caused by the man walking by her side. "Yes, I definitely need to get back."

"But we're just getting to know—"

Trinity sped up, snagging her shoe in her dress in her clumsy attempt to get away. She tripped and flung out her hand to catch herself.

Without warning, she found herself engulfed in musky male scent and heat. Her body froze, but her instincts knew exactly what they wanted. She breathed deep, sucking in the hint of cologne and the savory scent of him, imprinting his essence on her lungs.

Immediately guilt snaked through her. She pushed

against his arms, needing to be free. But he didn't release her until she was once again steady on her feet.

"Please don't," she gasped, recognizing her response to him with rising fear. Attraction by itself, let alone to a man she knew nothing about, was the last thing she needed in her life.

Unfazed by her protests, Rhett simply arched a brow as he pulled back. "I assumed from our talk that you didn't care for a crowd."

Puzzled, she said, "Yes?"

"Well, if your hand had hit right there—" his gaze turned to the wall where she would have landed, right on the frame of one of the beloved portraits in the rotunda "—then you would have set off the alarm and brought a whole load of people running."

And caused an epic scene being found in the arms of another man six weeks after her husband's death. Her cheeks burned as she imagined it. She quickly covered them with her palms. What a nightmare.

"Thank you," she choked out, unable to look up into Rhett's gray-green gaze.

But he was having none of that. He tucked firm fingers under her chin and lifted her face, displacing her own hands covering her embarrassment. Then he removed his arm from her, creating a small, intimate space between them.

Then she felt his thumb rub against the fullness of her bottom lip. A jolt of electricity shot through her. His eyelids lowered, and he gave her a slumberous, searching look that sent aftershocks down her spine.

"My pleasure," he said quietly. Then he was gone.

* * *

"So I see you've met our little gold digger."

Something about Richard Hyatt's voice always hit Rhett like nails on a chalkboard. Suppressing a wince took effort. He turned to find the heavyset man standing behind him, years of self-indulgence stamped on his pale, bloated face. His wife stood beside him, looking like his polar opposite. From the first moment Rhett had met with them, the couple had reminded him of the Jack Sprat nursery rhyme. Patricia Hyatt was pencil thin and her expression remained hard no matter the topic of conversation.

Somehow Rhett couldn't imagine the pale, vulnerable woman he'd met in the rotunda marrying into a family that included these people, but appearances could be deceiving…as Rhett knew better than most. He'd been on the receiving end of dishonest treachery more times than he could count, personally and professionally, but it was his ability to look beneath the surface of a pretty face and find the hidden ugliness that made him a master at his job.

Well, he preferred to consider it a true calling.

Trinity appeared genuinely innocent, from her wide, doe-brown eyes to the emotions that had flitted through her expression when she'd thought she was alone. There was a purity to her beauty that drew him in, urged him to let his guard down and believe that she'd been a true bride to Richard's deceased nephew, not a grifter. There was also something about her that woke sensations that weren't usually a part of his investigations.

But crying in public when there was any chance she might get caught? That had his Spidey senses tingling.

Was she simply a great actress? Had she taken advantage of Michael Hyatt and caught an unexpected win when he died so suddenly? Had she wormed her way into his bed, then into his will? From what he'd been told, that seductive innocence was a lie…and it was Rhett's responsibility to prove it.

Still, something about the whole scenario didn't quite fit. Rhett's instincts were usually spot-on from the moment he met someone. But with Trinity, the signal seemed to be intermittent. Not that he would be voicing that suspicion to his new client.

"Do you think it's wise to be speaking with me tonight?" he asked before indulging in a miniscule sip from his whiskey glass. Normally, he didn't drink on a job, but he did need to look the part in tonight's crowd. And blending in, playing the part, was something at which Rhett was extremely skilled. He glanced around, noting that Trinity hadn't returned to mingle in the crowd yet. But if she did, he wanted this meeting to look as casual as possible.

"Just a brief chat," Richard said, his gaze shifting back and forth over the surrounding crowd in a way that was blatantly suspicious. He extended a meaty hand. "You know how to make it look like a first meeting, don't you?"

Rhett smothered a sigh before shaking the other man's hand. Working with amateurs who thought they knew everything was such a pain in the ass.

"Of course," he said, his tone smooth and his voice

pitched low. "It's nice to meet you, Mr. Hyatt. I had the pleasure of meeting Trinity Hyatt moments ago."

Richard smirked, as if pleased Rhett had taken his direction, but Patricia snapped, "Don't call her that. I will never acknowledge that woman's so-called marriage to my nephew. Ever."

She might not, but that didn't mean the law wouldn't. Rhett didn't bother making the distinction. That was their lawyer's job.

"Regardless, our meeting was quite satisfactory. I don't foresee any problems with proceeding."

Satisfied smiles appeared on Richard's and Patricia's faces. As much as the Hyatts' obvious greed for their deceased nephew's estate left a bad taste in Rhett's mouth, he couldn't deny their suspicions had basis in reality. Trinity Romero had become Trinity Hyatt a mere week before her new husband had died in a helicopter crash, taking her from a lowly administrator at one of her husband's charities to a very wealthy widow. A claim her new family was already protesting in court. She did have a handwritten copy of his new will, but her lawyer insisted the official copy had been with her husband in the helicopter he'd died in on his way to his lawyer's office.

*Convenient.*

"I knew you were the man for the job," Richard was saying. "Our lawyer knew exactly who to turn to. A man like you will make her putty in your hands in a week—"

"Maybe less," his wife murmured, eyeing Rhett in a most unladylike way over the rim of her wineglass.

Richard ignored her. "You'll get the truth from her, then we will have evidence for our court case. Anything to put this whole debacle behind us."

"Remember, I cannot guarantee that time frame, Mr. Hyatt."

Richard's ham-handed slap on the back left Rhett uncomfortable but he knew better than to show it. Clients were never happy if you gave any hint of not trusting them.

The pat was accompanied by a hearty, "I have full faith in you, my man. And it seems like others are starting to get on board."

Rhett knew what Richard was referring to, as anyone in his position should, but still asked, "Meaning?"

"Apparently New Orleans' resident gossip blogger, one of those anonymous channels that dishes all the dirt, has started digging into Trinity's secrets. That should help our cause," he said with an overly loud guffaw. "Our lawyer will send you a link before the meeting tomorrow."

Again, Rhett didn't let on that he knew about the gossip column. He was nothing if not thorough. No single thing was left to chance. Rhett had seen the alert just as soon as the post had gone live. *NOLA Secrets & Scandals* was exceedingly popular in the city and gaining ground across the South. In less than three months, the Instagram page connected with the blog had gained over 100,000 followers. It had caught on not just with gossipmongers, but within the upper classes, who relished knowing and spreading the secret tidbits the blogger exposed.

Rhett shifted a little in his jacket, for once wishing he'd sent his partner, Chris, instead of taking this job

himself. But Chris had his hands full with a case involv-
ing a gigolo trying to swindle an elderly woman out of
her fortune; Chris's job was to seduce the old lady right
out from under him so her children would ultimately
receive their rightful inheritance.

On the surface, what their company did sounded
down and dirty, but it really wasn't. They might whisper a few sweet words or hold someone a little closer
than publicly proper, but there was a line that was never
crossed. A line that Rhett had never wanted to cross.
After all, he'd had enough betrayal in his life without
deliberately putting himself into a situation that could
only have a bad ending.

They were coming down to the wire on that case, but
Rhett couldn't wait for Chris to wrap it up. Oh, Rhett
could certainly do this job. Trinity's beauty eased any
hardship caused by her gauche in-laws. Just the thought
of the hunt, the subtle maneuvers required to ferret out
the information he needed to undermine any claim she
had on the Hyatt estate set his blood pumping.

He just had to ignore the other things about Trinity
that made his heart pound.

As his new clients eased off with a casual wave and
a not-so-subtle wink, Rhett indulged in the barest sip
of his whiskey. He casually zeroed in on the very spot
where Trinity was standing. He'd known the moment
she'd reentered the museum's grand ballroom. His brain
had registered every glance she'd thrown his way, no
matter how much she'd tried to hide it. So he let the dis-
taste he'd felt for his clients' motives show momentarily

on his face. He wanted her to see that he'd met her in-laws and didn't care for them that much.

He could almost feel her curiosity and concern across the space between them.

Now he let himself make eye contact, then he lifted his glass in her direction, catching her wide-eyed surprise as he acknowledged a connection neither of them had put into words. Regardless of what her in-laws might say, what society might whisper or what his own conscience might condemn, getting to know each other was going to be a very sure pleasure.

# Two

Trinity tried not to be alarmed by the number of people seated around the table at the emergency board meeting of Hyatt Heights, Inc. *It looked like a world peace negotiation instead of a business meeting.*

There were the lawyers: stone-faced as they set up their laptops. There were the businessmen: some familiar and friendly faces, some not so much. Then there were Richard and his wife, Patricia, whose faces had never been friendly in all the years she'd known them.

They'd never pretended to love Michael, though he was their only nephew. Instead they'd spent all their time complaining to him about Hyatt Heights losing money and the waste of running *Maison de Jardin.* The home for abused women and children had become Mi-

chael's life passion after his parents had been killed in
a car accident in his midtwenties.

That was when Michael's unlikely friendship with Trinity had started. They'd both been dealing with the repercussions of losing their families, though in different ways.
Trinity as a victim of violence who found shelter with her
mother at *Maison de Jardin*. Michael as the rescuer who
took them in and gave them hope and a future. It had led
to a lifetime connection that had shaped her entire world.

Trinity forced her thoughts back to the present, rather
than let herself get lost in the bittersweet memories of
her best friend. Despite the comfort they gave her, she
somehow knew she needed all her focus on the here and
now. People didn't just call an emergency board meeting for any old reason, right?

*Those darn posts…* They had to have something to
do with it.

"Doing okay, Trinity?" Bill LeBlanc asked from her
right side.

She gave him a small smile, grateful to have the one
other person who had known her husband as well as she
had by her side through all of this. An old-fashioned
Southern lawyer in his ever-present vest and bowtie,
Bill looked right at home amid the arched windows and
wainscoting of the boardroom at Hyatt House, the private
mansion from which Michael Hyatt had run his business
and charitable foundation. Bill's only regret was that,
as Michael's lawyer, he hadn't been able to finalize the
will before Michael's death. But he was doing all that he
could to help Trinity honor his client and friend's wishes.

"I feel completely unprepared," she said low, not

wanting anyone else in the room to overhear. There were a few people here who would jump on any weakness like sharks scenting blood in the water.

What she needed was a strategy. Being perceived as a strong leader by the board of Hyatt Heights was essential. If she inherited Michael's position, she would be CEO of the corporation, and a majority shareholder, but still needed the board on her side to put through the initiatives and decisions that could be supported by the other shareholders.

An injunction had created a temporary board director to serve in Michael's place during the court case, while Trinity still handled Michael's other businesses and whatever tasks the temporary board director asked of her. So she and Richard were "auditioning" while the case was ongoing. If she didn't prove her worth, Trinity could still lose the CEO position, though the shares would remain hers through inheritance.

Which would make carrying out Michael's wishes even harder. The two board meetings she'd attended since her husband's death had included talking points and presentations and charts that Bill had briefed her on before they'd arrived.

Not today. There'd been no preparation, no warnings. Trinity knew on an intellectual level that she needed to focus on getting through this without hinting how much she was out of her depth. She was a smart woman, but her crash course in billion-dollar businesses over the last two months had been steep.

Plus, her sleep last night had been repeatedly interrupted by the image of bright gray-green eyes that left her restless and needy in a way she'd never felt before. A way she was definitely not comfortable with.

"It will be fine," Bill assured her as the meeting was called to order.

Richard Hyatt sat with his wife and lawyer at an angle across from Trinity and Bill, which should have been enough to put her out of their line of sight. Still she shifted in discomfort as she noticed the couple's gazes trained in her direction. What trouble were they stirring up now?

She had to wonder what influence Richard had used with the temporary board director to get everyone to show up for this. He acted as if winning the case for Michael's inheritance was a done deal and he'd already been elevated to CEO, instead of still being only a member of the board.

"This meeting at my request to the chair was called with some urgency to address issues brought to my awareness this morning," Richard said, taking to his feet as if to assert his superiority over the others around the table. "How many of you have seen this?"

He clicked a button on the remote in his hand, which caused a portion of the back wall to slide down. The large screen behind it was already on, displaying a photo of Trinity. She could easily read the headline on the screen.

### Suspicious Widow Fights for Control of Hyatt Estate

Trinity couldn't hold in a gasp, though she would have given anything not to react after Richard smirked in her direction.

But he didn't stop there. "I told the board you'd be bad for business, but they wouldn't listen."

His words were lost in the cacophony of voices as board members asserted their opinions. They clicked on the keyboards before them on the table's highly polished surface. He'd gotten his point across, and that was all that mattered.

Trinity pressed her shaking fingers together. The headline and blog post were only the beginning of the ugliness. There were also photos. The series of pictures included one of her at the funeral, one from the charity event the night before looking particularly standoffish, and a picture of her marriage certificate. She tuned out the noise around her as she read the short captions and comments.

They included vague claims about how unfit Trinity was, simply because she'd never been part of New Orleans's upper crust and ran a charity for a living. There were specific details about her short marriage to Michael and a link to documentation about the court case filed by Richard and Patricia, all under the hashtag #NOLASecrets. A few Black Widow comments thrown in didn't sit well with her either.

"Where is this from?" Bill's sharp voice jolted her from her absorption. She'd assumed he knew about the rumors making the social media rounds.

"That new gossip blogger who's all the rage at the moment," Patricia said. "Everyone who is anyone is following her blog and other social media." Her eye roll was almost comical.

Another board member interrupted, his voice sounding panicky. "It's only a matter of time before this hits other news sites. *NOLA Secrets & Scandals* is really making waves."

"It already has," Richard said, his voice calm. There was an ominous glint of satisfaction in his gaze as he trained it once again on Trinity. "Our stock has already begun to drop."

There was a flurry of rustling as phones were pulled from pockets and briefcases. Those with laptops began furiously clicking. The murmurs grew louder as the board members confirmed for themselves what Richard had said.

Bill scoffed, looking up from his own phone. "We have no idea whether this was caused by that hatchet piece. The stock is barely down from yesterday."

"Mark my words, it's going to fall, and fall fast," Richard assured him. "I mean, look at this post." He clicked on a link in the sidebar. The headline read, "Suspicious Marriage Threatens Local Jobs." Then the next line, "And it's all her fault."

Trinity allowed herself to blink slowly once, twice, before saying, "I thought you said it was the blogger's fault."

"There wouldn't even be a post if it wasn't for you. Obviously, *they* agree it's your fault, too."

"You don't even know who wrote this," Trinity argued, though she knew it was futile.

"The public doesn't care, little girl. Shareholders just read the news and start dumping their stock. Prices go down. People lose jobs."

Bill interrupted with, "This isn't news. It's rumors. Once the truth comes out in court—"

"When?" Richard demanded. "In a year? Two years? How much damage will be done in that amount of time?"

Trinity's heart picked up speed.

That's when Richard and Patricia's lawyer saw an opening. "Let's not forget that if the stock drops, you might all be booted off the board."

Larry Pelegrine, one of the men who had been kind enough to answer Trinity's questions over the last six weeks, spoke up. "Now, we can't allow this to get out of hand. Not because of how it might affect any one of us individually," he said with gentlemanly emphasis, without directly pointing out the crass slant of the lawyer's words, "but because of the thousands of people who work for the Hyatt companies. They have families to support. Families that need groceries and health insurance and—"

"We get it," Patricia said, her voice turning snide. "We need to help people...and ourselves."

How in the world could the other board members not see just how focused Richard and Patricia Hyatt were on bettering themselves, without caring about the effect of their actions on others? Or that their selfishness was the exact opposite of Michael's vision for his companies and charitable foundation?

Larry leaned forward. "Look, as much as I hate to say it, the reality is that if the company's valuation goes down, people *will* lose their jobs. And that valuation is partially reliant on how the outside world views the company, regardless of the truth."

The rest of the board members nodded and muttered to each other. Bill cast a sympathetic glance in Trinity's direction. She pressed her palms against her thighs beneath the protection of the table's edge. She and Bill and even Larry had worked hard to promote her abilities and skills to the rest of the board for the last six weeks. After all, she'd single-handedly run *Maison de Jardin* for Michael since she was twenty-three. It wasn't a small operation, by any stretch of the imagination, though it was miniscule compared to the entire Hyatt Heights operation.

She could feel the understanding and support they'd been working so hard to cultivate slowly sinking out from underneath her like sand beneath a wave on the beach. Once the court case was settled, the winner would own the largest portion of the company and would most likely be the CEO, giving them the most sway with the board. She needed them to believe in her, so she could use her power for the things Michael would have wanted. Richard had his own seat, but no true power if he didn't inherit Michael's estate.

One voice rose above the rest. "We have to do something."

Trinity was bombarded with questions and comments from all sides. She slowly drew in a breath, trying to think amid the chaos.

"I think this will help everyone see what I mean," Richard said.

This time he clicked to display a file. At first when

Trinity looked at the handout, the figures and columns jumbled before her eyes; then, she started to sort through the data. She could see Bill doing the same out of her peripheral vision. The negative projections on how their workforce and revenue would be impacted by the bad press hit Trinity hard.

No matter how much she told herself that this wasn't her fault, that what had simply started as a favor to her best friend had gotten completely out of control with his unexpected death, it didn't make her feel any less responsible for what could happen to innocent people along the way.

Patricia drove the nail in harder. "That's an estimated five thousand people with families in New Orleans alone who will end up unemployed."

A city in desperate need of jobs. Trinity knew that.

"You don't know that," Bill asserted, a little of his spirit reappearing.

The woman didn't seem to care about a little thing like facts...or decorum. She leaned forward, hands planted squarely on the table, and looked Trinity directly in the eye. "That means they're gonna need all the charity they can get. You know, the same kind your clients receive over at *Maison*," she said, a snide twist to her voice. "That's something your brain can actually grasp, right?"

Trinity felt herself withdraw from the unexpected attack, but forced herself to hold completely still. It was the only coping mechanism she had. If she held still, no one could see her, no one could take a swipe at her. Or in this case, gather any more evidence to use against her.

She forced her voice to stay steady as she said, "The last thing I want is for families to lose their income."

"They will as long as you hang this board up with your court case."

Trinity raised a brow in disbelief. "I'm not the one who initiated the case."

"That's not how the press sees it." Richard nodded toward the screen .

Larry stood up, his height and girth commanding attention. "Let's focus here. We need to do something about this before it gets to be a huge problem. The issue here is the need to sway public opinion in such a way that it will reassure our investors and raise stock prices." He sighed. "I believe I've got an idea."

His glance in her direction was almost apologetic. "Even before this bad press, I looked into a business consultant to help you. Now I realize hiring him might reassure our investors that our corporation is not simply being run by someone completely inexperienced."

Bill grunted, but Trinity laid a hand on his arm. Let everyone think she was inexperienced. She was, to a certain extent, though years spent talking aspects of his business through with Michael had taught her some very valuable things. Not that she'd expected to ever have to use that knowledge. But now that he was gone, she was more than grateful.

"That sounds like an interesting proposition," she said instead of rejecting the proposal outright.

"He's here, actually. He was in town and I asked if he would meet with you," Larry said.

That took her back a little bit, but at least it expedited things.

"Here?" Richard asked, his voice booming in the room. "Let's bring him in."

Trinity winced. How lovely—another businessman to "fix" the problem of her inexperience. Even if she won the case against the people trying to take her inheritance away, consultants like this would be telling her what to do.

The room went oddly quiet as Larry stepped out into the hallway. Trinity felt a sick kind of anticipation build inside her. Logic said if this consultant could help, it would be a good thing for a lot of people. Fear said he could end up being just one more person to criticize her after analyzing her every move.

The door opened and Larry stepped back inside with another man following close behind.

Trinity took one look into the gray-green eyes she'd never expected to see again and wished the floor would open up and swallow her whole.

Rhett saw the surprise in Trinity's eyes as he walked into the room but didn't experience the usual thrill he felt as the game started in earnest.

Angry tones and placating words swirled around the periphery of his awareness. Still Rhett couldn't tear his gaze from the wide-eyed woman seated halfway up the table. Her slender elegance seemed out of place amid the stout men in power suits who filled the room. Today her wealth of dark hair was pulled back from the fine cheekbones, making Rhett wish to see it loose and

tumbling in waves around her shoulders as it had last
night at the museum.

Today her expression was more guarded. He sensed
the hard barrier she'd placed between herself and those
she surely saw as adversaries, giving her the calm, blank
stare of a sphinx. Where had she learned to do that? Or
did it come naturally to her? Was it always her reaction
to the men surrounding her?

Or had he truly caught her in an unguarded moment
the night before, a time when she'd been alone with her
thoughts and unprepared to defend herself against her
enemies?

Rhett wasn't sure, but the question came from somewhere deep inside of him. It wasn't just curiosity about
information that would help him do his job. No, this
was a bone-deep desire to solve the mystery in front of
him. Would he be satisfied with exposing her as a liar?
Or would finding evidence of her less-than-stellar character leave him with a bad taste in his mouth for once?

Because Rhett wasn't just good at what he did. He
was exceptional. He had yet to complete a case without finding something to prove his client's suspicions
valid. This one would end the same…even if the chase
was much more interesting.

As Larry introduced Rhett to the board, Trinity
blinked, slowly, almost deliberately, then turned her
gaze toward the man seated beside her. Her lawyer,
Rhett remembered now from his files. Something about
her breaking eye contact with him finally jump-started
his adrenaline.

"I don't see how this will help," Bill complained.

"Why would his presence sway public opinion at all? It just looks like a PR move, which will hardly be reassuring."

"He has a proven track record of inspiring confidence in investors," Larry countered. Rhett had met the man earlier this morning, when Richard and Patricia had filled Larry in on Rhett's secret assignment. "We tell the media and our shareholders that we're addressing the concerns of our employees and making sure the business is in the best possible hands."

Protests rose around the room once more; the group sounded more like unruly schoolchildren than business professionals. Only Trinity sat quietly in the midst of the chaos.

It didn't take long for Rhett to reach his limit. He gave the black tabletop before him a firm smack. Once the room quieted and he had the full attention of those around him, he asked in a firm tone, "Do you want to make the best of this situation or lose everything you helped Michael Hyatt work so hard to build?"

The room went utterly still as Rhett deliberately moved his gaze from one man to the next. Even the background hum of the air conditioner seemed to subside. Then his attention fell on Trinity.

Her gaze was trained solely on him; she ignored everyone else. Something about her attention shook his control for a moment.

Startled at her reaction, he deliberately pulled his mental barriers back in place, then moved effortlessly into the spiel he had prepared to convince the board of his usefulness to their present dilemma. His cover story as a business consultant rolled smoothly off his tongue.

A brief discussion ensued, one Trinity continued to follow with that sphinxlike expression on her face. He knew she was soaking it all in, but she showed very little reaction to his pitch. Until the end.

When he was done speaking, she stood up. It wasn't an attempt to intimidate, as he'd seen the other men do earlier in the meeting through the small spy camera Richard was carrying for him. No. Instead, tranquility radiated from her, garnering the attention of those around her.

Rhett didn't understand what that magnetism was, but he was determined to find out.

All eyes were riveted on her as she said in a solid voice that held no hint of hesitation, "Welcome, Mr. Brannon. We appreciate your willingness to take on our unusual situation."

He heard a quickly stifled hiss from Patricia, but Rhett didn't look her way. He found himself too fascinated with this new, unexpected side of Trinity, this authority that seemed to come naturally to her. The woman he'd met last night had been hesitant. Shy, even. In this moment, she was commanding.

For the first time, he wondered why the Hyatts saw Trinity as more of a nuisance who stood in their way rather than a true threat. They should be much more concerned. Because his instincts said he was now facing someone who might prove to be a more than competent adversary when crossed.

"Gentlemen," she said, her tone brooking no argument, "there's been enough discussion for today. I believe hiring Mr. Brannon as a consultant is an acceptable solution all around."

She glanced toward the interim board director, who nodded. "This meeting is adjourned. You all know your way out," he said.

As one, everyone stood and headed toward the door. Not a single person lingered. Rhett could see why. Trinity had closed the discussion with a force of personality that hadn't been in evidence earlier.

His spy camera hadn't caught her saying very much in the meeting, but that didn't mean she hadn't made an impact. It was almost as if she'd sat in the room, blending in like an old-fashioned wallflower, while she soaked in every word being said. But when she'd made her decision, it was time for everyone else to get the hell out of Dodge, so to speak.

Impressive.

Whispering among themselves, the crowd, led by Richard and his wife, filed out the door held open by a butler. Rhett would have gotten lost in the sprawling mansion if not for the butler leading the way.

It possessed an opulent, dark beauty in the curved arches of every window, the elaborately carved entryways and myriad displays of art and books in every nook and cranny. Quintessentially Southern, it reflected the rich, spicy atmosphere of the city with splashes of bright color and nods to the rich, turbulent history of the land.

Gorgeous, but stifling. Did Trinity find the elegance oppressive? Her focus on her responsibilities, while admirable on the surface, could simply be part of the act. Dutiful widow and all. Would she welcome him into her confidence to help her with the duties she'd inherited, even as he gathered the evidence to take her down? Though it was just an assignment, his heartbeat gained speed at the thought of working so closely with her.

No, he needed to proceed with caution. He needed to get close to her, yes. But only to do his job. He needed the real motive…not the real woman.

Still, enticing Trinity to have a little fun could serve his purpose well.

Trinity exchanged a few quiet words with her lawyer when Bill paused beside her, but she didn't move as he headed on through the door. Rhett didn't miss the hard look Bill threw his way. That man would have a background check completed before the end of today. Too bad he would only find what Rhett wanted him to know.

Somehow, without the words being spoken, Rhett knew Trinity expected him to remain behind. Sheer curiosity held him still. He was psyched to see what other surprises she had in store for him.

As his gaze returned to her, he caught the briefest of moments when her whole body seemed weighed down. Her shoulders drooped. Her head hung forward a few inches. Her expression was lined with despair. It was only there for a moment, as if the demands of speaking earlier had drained every last inch of her energy.

Then the moment disappeared, and she was once more closed off to his prying eyes.

As soon as the last board member cleared the room, Trinity nodded to the butler and he firmly closed the carved wooden doors. Not missing a beat, she turned to Rhett and fixed him with her gaze.

"Tell me exactly what game it is you think you're playing, Mr. Brannon."

# Three

Watching Rhett's gray eyes widen with shock was even better than the special scenes in the movies that were her big indulgence now that she was an adult. Her mother had believed films were sinful, but Trinity had no such hang-ups. There was nothing better than losing herself in scene after colorful scene…except maybe throwing Rhett off guard by stepping outside of the carefully constructed box he'd obviously placed her in.

She had a feeling he wasn't often at a loss for words. Today his presence was even more commanding than last night. He'd stepped into a room full of powerful businessmen without any hesitation. He'd taken up the reins of the meeting as if he'd been born to lead and established his abilities with just a few simple words.

This was a version of the man she'd met last night.

Still gorgeous in that glossy-magazine way, but without the flirtatiousness and single-minded intensity of the night before. Today he'd been performing for the entire room. Last night he'd been focused only on her.

Or so it had seemed.

What was he really up to? She needed answers.

"You knew who I was last night." The words weren't a question, because they both knew the truth. She waited for the excuses to start rolling in.

"Trinity."

His deep voice held the same intimate tone that it had the night before, except now they were in a boardroom, instead of what had seemed like a very private meeting of their own. Still she had to suppress a shiver as her skin prickled.

This time it was her turn to be taken off guard. His dark good looks, the pull of his powerful personality sucked her under. What was the point in asking questions? It would be easier to sit and stare for a while, let his sexy energy distract her from the truth that had to be lurking behind that charming smile. It would be such a relief to drop the suspicions and defenses the situation seemed to require.

"You're right," he said, the ready confession surprising her. "I did recognize you—after you told me your name."

That made sense. The story of Michael's death and her inheritance had certainly been in the news lately. "It still didn't occur to you to introduce yourself? Your real self?"

One thing Trinity had learned in life was that you

never got anywhere if you kept backing down…and she wasn't moving forward with this plan until she had some answers.

"Well, yes," he conceded.

His gaze dipped, making her suddenly aware of her arms crossed over her front and how defensive she must seem. She forced herself to relax, but that seemed to warrant another quick look from him, one that lingered just long enough to cause gooseflesh to break out over her forearms.

"But?" she prompted. *Eyes up, bucko.*

"But I wasn't sure whether this plan had been shared with *you* yet. Besides, I didn't know the job was definite until this morning. I just flew in last night. It was simply…a tentative offer."

His logic was perfectly reasonable. He'd been right to wonder. After all, she hadn't been told why he was here…or that he was here at all. Something she couldn't fault him for, as much as she'd like to.

So why did her suspicions linger?

It didn't help that a slight smile graced his lips, almost as if he were amused by all the questions. Defensiveness rose inside her, a desire to build a protective wall around herself, so he couldn't see or touch or know any part of her that might tell him just a little too much about the real Trinity Hyatt.

This was *business only.*

She forced herself to focus on that. "Why would you come here just to consult in a situation like this?"

He shrugged. "It's what I do. Teaching people to run their businesses properly, or more efficiently, or simply to evaluate and suggest new processes. People who inherit businesses like you have are sometimes more in need of those services than most."

"Isn't that kind of like 'those who can't do, teach'?"

That sounded rude when she said it out loud, but maybe she wanted to push him away. Just a little.

"Not when you're as good at it as I am."

He said the words with a perfectly straight face. So why did she feel like he was insinuating something that had nothing to do with business?

Determined to distract him, not to mention herself, she asked, "Do you usually conduct business by lying to people? The people you're supposed to be helping?"

He straightened, though his facial expression didn't change. "I wasn't lying. I just didn't reveal everything right when we met because nothing had been decided upon."

Warning bells went off in Trinity's head at his dangerous logic. They got even louder as he leaned over, resting his hands against the edge of the boardroom table, a wide smile appearing on his lips.

Why did her heart speed up, just like it had earlier? They were only talking. She knew Bill, Richard and the butler, Frederick, were just outside. Frederick wouldn't leave her unguarded with a stranger. There wasn't any danger here. But the response had to be fear…right?

Then Rhett spoke. "Besides, I definitely didn't want to kill the mood with something as boring as business."

"If I had known—" Trinity sputtered.

"You never would have spoken to me about art or beauty or feelings last night," he finished for her. "All of it would have been off the table." He leaned a little closer. "While I appreciate what you're saying, I simply wasn't ready to break the mood."

Implying he'd felt all or more of the attraction she had as they'd stood alone in the rotunda. But she had been willing to walk away because discussing those things with him made her feel much more than she should. Regardless of the fact that her husband had only been dead six weeks, and the fact that getting involved with anyone would give the press one more reason to flay her alive, Trinity was fully aware that she wasn't experienced enough to handle a man like Rhett.

He had the sophistication of a man who knew exactly what he wanted and exactly how to get it. She was completely naive by comparison—she knew that. Could she work with the businessman to stabilize the situation at the company and still give the fascinating charismatic version of Rhett a wide berth?

She glanced down at his hands resting on the tabletop and frowned. She had to establish the rules as strictly as she could. It was up to her to set the tone, stake the boundaries.

"Just how much is this consulting job going to cost me?" She had no doubt that this would come out of her portion of the inheritance.

He frowned, as if he disapproved of her attempt to bring the focus back to business. But he didn't back down. Instead, he gestured toward the scattered papers still littering the slick black surface of the conference table. "Does it really matter?"

As much as she hated to admit it, he was right. She

wasn't in a place where she could bargain...not when the livelihoods of over 5,000 people were at stake.

When they left the boardroom, Rhett could feel Richard approaching them. Even if he hadn't been looking, Rhett would have known by the way Trinity straightened. The way she gathered herself gave her almost another inch in height. Was she readying herself in defense...or to go on the offensive?

Relief spread through him as Bill arrived, too, so Trinity wasn't alone with Richard. Her feelings weren't something he should care about—as a matter of fact, the more uncomfortable she was, the more likely she was to make a mistake. Which was to his advantage.

So why was he worrying about her so much?

His phone vibrated. Rhett glanced at the display before excusing himself.

"Rhett here," he said, connecting the call after walking a few feet away.

It was his standard greeting for his business partner, a signal to Chris that Rhett had to be careful about his words because someone might overhear him.

Once he was at a safe distance, he turned back around and met Trinity's gaze. She didn't immediately look away.

Chris's voice distracted him. "What's this I hear about you wanting me to take over your job? Has some woman got you whupped already?"

"In twenty-four hours?" His partner was way off base, though Rhett had the uncomfortable feeling this job wasn't going to follow his usual patterns.

"Well, it could happen," Chris said.

"In what universe?" The ribbing had the familiar comfort of a worn pair of jeans, calming Rhett's concerns.

"Stefan was really worried. He said you sounded funny on the phone," Chris said. "I figured lust must have hit hard and quick."

"I'm impervious." At least, he hoped so.

"That's what they all say."

Picking up the cue, Rhett and Chris said in unison, "But for us it's the truth."

"Seriously, Rhett," Chris said, his tone finally turning serious, "what's the problem?"

Rhett was silent for a moment, unsure how much to get into. In addition to the trio standing nearby, several board members still lingered across the anteroom near the impressive arched window. "Nothing I can't handle. Last night was weird but I'm over it."

"That was quick."

Oh, the odd premonitions he'd had about Trinity were still there, but Rhett refused to cave into his feelings. "I've got it under control."

"You sure?" Chris asked.

"Yeah. I have no doubt I'm gonna find something here. It's just a matter of digging deep enough." It always was.

"Just be careful you don't enjoy it too much."

Though the warning came with the territory, Rhett felt it on a much deeper level than usual. "I know better than to get involved."

"Hey, we all need a reminder sometimes. We were

made to be cynical. Sometimes we just listen to our man parts more than our common sense."

Rhett knew better than to protest. That would just make him sound defensive.

Apparently, silence made him sound guilty, too, because Chris kept up his lecture.

"If it was just one time, life would be different. You and I both would be different," Chris said. "But we were exposed to the truth too many times. Never forget your dad and Veronica…or Mickey and Tracy…or even Lily and—"

"Uncle Joe," they said together. They'd had this discussion many times before. Both of them had families littered with betrayal. Every couple Chris mentioned was an example. It had been a training ground for the work Rhett now did.

"Dude," Chris went on. "Anastasia taught you well."

The mention of his former fiancée was just another reminder for Rhett to harden his resolve. He was fully aware of how dangerous lust could be to a man. Especially when he was staring at the incredible silhouette of Trinity from behind. Her height might be an inch or two below average, but her curves were fully present and accounted for…

And he was accounting for each and every one. He needed to take Chris's words to heart and get his head in the game. "Roger that," he said before signing off.

Now Rhett could move on to the next stage in his plan to insinuate himself into Trinity's life.

He approached the little group just in time to hear Richard say, "At least you're being sensible. It won't do any of us any good if you ruin everything before we take over."

"If you take over," Bill countered with a stern glance.

Richard smirked. "It's only a matter of time."

Trinity held still, not reacting to the men's conversation, though her gaze remained on Richard's face long enough for the man to actually fidget in his designer leather shoes. *Impressive.*

"A little snag," Rhett said, raising his phone to indicate the call.

"Anything we can do to help?" Bill asked with a lawyer's version of a polite smile.

Rhett hoped so. "Can you recommend a place to stay? My secretary said the hotel wasn't able to extend my reservation because of a convention or something."

Bill frowned in concentration, but Richard didn't think for a moment. "You don't need a hotel."

To Rhett's fascination, Trinity showed her first touch of annoyance by pressing her full lips firmly together. Was she holding back a protest for what she could see coming? How would she feel if she knew he and Richard had arranged this ahead of time?

*Doesn't matter, numbskull.*

"You can stay right here," Richard replied gleefully. "Hyatt House has plenty of guest rooms. Right, Trinity?"

When Trinity replied, she spoke with a little too much control. "Of course. There's plenty of space here."

"And it will save you a few dollars, too," Richard added.

"I'm a little more concerned with how others might

view Mr. Brannon living here with me, since I'm so recent a widow—"

"Please, call me Rhett."

"You don't have a reputation to protect, anyway." Richard just had to step in one more time. Did the man have no tact?

Once again Trinity's face went completely still at Richard Hyatt's insult.

"Richard," Bill rumbled in warning.

But Rhett ignored his secret employer and focused entirely on Trinity. He clasped her fragile hand in his and raised it to his lips in an old-fashioned gesture. This gave him the opportunity to watch her guarded expression crack just enough, her eyes widening as his lips met her skin. He allowed only the briefest of touches before he pulled back and said, "Don't you worry. I understand my job here, and my expertise is completely at your disposal."

Confusion mingled with caution in her expression. Not letting his satisfaction show as she puzzled over the double meaning of his words, he went on, "You have my word that my behavior will be completely professional. The gossips would find me completely boring."

For once, Rhett wasn't sure that was a promise he could keep.

# Four

$W$hy did walking down the hall, Rhett at her back, make Trinity so uncomfortable?

Not in the sense of being scared. It was more of an awareness that he was watching her, moving with her, that sifted through her skin into her very consciousness. It was craziness. She didn't know this man at all. Keeping her distance was the best option, especially considering she'd be working with him starting today.

She couldn't get away.

She knew for a fact that there was only one room ready at a moment's notice inside Hyatt House, and it was directly across the hall from her bedroom.

So much for keeping her distance.

Rhett's voice interrupted her obsessive thoughts. "I

appreciate you letting me stay here on such short notice," he said.

So polite. Why was he being this nice to her? He had to be working with the enemy. That thought stopped her in her tracks, and she whirled around to face him.

"Did Richard know why you were here before I did?" she demanded.

She caught an expression of surprise he probably didn't want her to see, considering how quickly it disappeared.

"I saw you speaking with him at the event last night."

Rhett was quiet for a moment longer than she expected, which made her want to squirm. But she refused to let herself. Now that she'd started on this road, there was no reason to back down.

Finally, he said, "I was introduced to him last night, but Larry was the one who initially contacted me. Look, I know this situation is highly unusual. You want to learn more about the businesses. Let me help you do that…and be seen doing it. For everyone's sake."

His words made sense. Still, she had to stay on guard. He was too convenient, too accommodating, too—attractive.

"How much can you teach me? And can you do it in enough time to make a difference with the press?"

He inclined his head, as if approving of her questions. "Right now, I'm at your disposal. Let's just evaluate where you are, what you'll need, and go from there. I have to know more about you."

"Why?"

"I need to know how you learn, what you need to learn, what will put you on the fast track to success."

"That sounds…" Trinity suddenly realized she was rubbing at her temple and forced her hand down to her side. What it sounded like was way too much one-on-one time with this man.

"Good, right? Trust me. This process will lead to good things."

That she wasn't so sure of. She only made it a few more feet down the hallway before gesturing to an open door. "This will be your room."

Rhett stepped to the door and glanced around before turning back.

But that gave her a few seconds to observe the way his suit jacket fit his wide shoulders. The slight curl of the black hair brushing his collar. The confident stance that said he was in control, even in these unfamiliar circumstances. She hated to admit her toes curled a little.

It had to be the weariness from all these weeks of constant turmoil, stress and being under observation. She was plumb worn-out, as her mother would say. That was all.

As he turned back to her, she adopted the most pleasant version of her hostess smile she could manage under the weight of the exhaustion slowly descending over her. "Your luggage will be brought up when it arrives. Luncheon will be on the back patio in an hour."

A tempting half smile appeared on his sculpted lips. "You don't have to feed me, too."

She spoke before thinking. "My mama would have a fit if I didn't feed a guest." Hearing her country twang peek through brought her up short. "Besides, it'll save me money, right?"

Wow. This exhaustion was weakening the very facade that had gotten her through the last six weeks. *Try again.* "I apologize. That was inappropriate of me."

"No. I understand where it came from."

Though she resisted it, she could feel both her body and spirit soften as he gifted her with a look of understanding. "Still, I apologize. My only excuse is I'm very tired. I would normally never make a guest feel unwelcome. Please join me for lunch."

"I imagine this has been a very stressful time for you." His hushed tone urged her to confide in him, and for just a moment, Trinity wanted to. She knew she couldn't, she most definitely shouldn't, but it was more tempting than she would admit to anyone.

Why was he saying all the right things? Trinity needed to get away from the whirling suspicions clouding her brain before her tightly held control cracked wide open.

"Let us know if you need anything to get settled in," she said as she slowly backed away.

"Thank you, Trinity."

The way he said her name had her scrambling across the hall to her own room and into the en suite bathroom. She had to get away. His gaze had been searching, seeing way more than made her comfortable.

With shaking hands, she opened the taps and let cool water run over her wrists. Closing her eyes, she refused to look into the mirror before her. What did Rhett see when he looked at her? A gold digger? A helpless widow about to ruin her dead husband's legacy? Someone pretending to be more capable than she was?

Then the more dangerous question: What did she want him to see?

That one she refused to wrap her head around.

Maybe it would be best to lie down for a little while before she had to face him again. Getting some rest might tamp down the mood swings and give her a more solid perspective. Normally Trinity was the one logical, proactive person in the room. She just needed a few minutes to process everything that had happened in the last twenty-four hours.

She reached above her head to remove the pins from her hair, breathing a sigh of relief as the weight fell from her scalp. Then she unbuttoned her suit jacket. As she walked back into the bedroom, she shook the heavy length out and pulled the hem of her camisole from the waistband of her skirt.

"Trinity, I—"

To her dismay, Rhett stood at the open door. His brows were raised high as he took in her disheveled appearance. Even though she was fully clothed, something about his look made her feel closer to naked than she'd ever been in a man's presence.

"What are you doing in here?" she demanded, pulling the two sides of her jacket closed in an attempt to feel more secure.

His gaze followed the gesture, then traveled up to her loose hair. He cleared his throat before saying, "I had a question and saw you come in here. The door was open."

He seemed reluctant to pull his gaze from her hair, but finally did look around the room. She knew what he would see. Michael had let her decorate it to her taste, so the room had the feel of an old-fashioned library, with an antique bed that matched the bookshelves lining half the room. There was a writing desk and feminine purple bedding and curtains. The room had made her incredibly happy when Michael had designed it for her.

Now she felt like her very self was being exposed from every corner…something she did not want Rhett to see. But he was too quick for her.

Finally, his gray-green gaze made its way back to her, the intensity bringing a burn of guilt to her cheeks. Though she wasn't quite sure what she had to feel guilty about…until he asked, "Is this your bedroom?"

With those words, she knew he'd guessed part of her secret. She could only pray he didn't guess it all.

There were so many questions Rhett had wanted to ask Trinity. So many things he wanted to know about her. Some of them involved business—which he would get to in good time. Many of them did not. He knew he had no true reason to dive deep into her personal life except insofar as it helped him build his clients' case. But that didn't stop the burn of curiosity low in his gut.

He kept their conversation as innocuous as possible during their quiet lunch together, not wanting to set her further on edge. Her stiff body language and wary glances when she first came to the table warned him that their time in her bedroom still upset her, even hours later. She hadn't wanted him to see her private space.

Or was that just an act for his benefit?

She very politely thanked the young lady who served their meal and very properly laid her silver and napkin in place for it to be easily removed. Genteel actions, but they felt learned. Had her husband taught her all the right moves? Had she learned them so she could earn her place when the time was right?

Why didn't Rhett want to believe that?

"We can work in my office," she said, her gesture for him to follow her quiet and elegant.

The questions continued as he followed her to the wing of the massive mansion that housed the business operations. Would Trinity have taken over her husband's office? She didn't appear to have shared the master bedroom with him.

The room she was sleeping in was too lived in, too much like *her* for her to have moved in a mere six weeks ago. No. It wasn't the room of a widow trying to get away from the memory of her dead husband. It was a room designed for her. That intrigued him most of all.

The Hyatts would find it intriguing, too, he was sure. Which meant Rhett had to figure out exactly what it meant.

He wouldn't be sharing anything just yet. When the time was right, he'd ask the questions nagging him, and hope he knew what to do with the answers.

Trinity led him through one of the elaborately carved oak doors into a room with high ceilings supported by numerous bookshelves. There was a heavy, polished desk with a clean desktop containing multiple computer screens, now dark.

Trinity kept walking through a side door where she paused beside the desk of a smiling woman with an air of quiet competence.

"Anything I need to see, Jenny?" Trinity asked.

The secretary frowned. "Well…"

"Besides that," Trinity said, wiggling her phone to indicate she'd already seen the posts.

"Sorry, Mrs. Hyatt," Jenny said.

Rhett watched the interaction with interest. The Hyatts would have everyone believe that Trinity was nothing but a gold digger. But the staff in the house seemed to be devoted to her, or at least friendly. Did they just know her better? Or had they been fooled?

"Jenny, this is Rhett Brannon. He's going to be helping me out with the businesses for the foreseeable future."

Rhett smiled as Jenny nodded an acknowledgment in his direction.

"Please have an office space set up for him across the hall."

"That's not necessary," he protested.

Trinity turned her sage gaze his way. "I want you to be comfortable here. That includes having your own space."

Was she buttering him up? Or was this genuine Louisiana hospitality?

Rhett smiled his thanks despite his questions and followed Trinity into the room beyond.

This office was a smaller, more feminine version of the one they'd left behind. It was also more old-school. Whereas Michael had appeared to be the epitome of a modern businessman who did the entirety of his work on his computer, the same could not be said of this office's occupant. Though Trinity had a monitor and keyboard, there were no other indications of expensive technology. Instead, the wall facing her desk appeared to have been taken over by an army of whiteboards. Each one seemed dedicated to aspects of Michael's businesses that she seemed to be tracking.

Personnel. Income. Expenditures. Contracts. Stock market numbers for the last week.

"Wow," he said, not realizing at first that he'd spoken aloud.

He turned back to where she stood behind the small but gorgeous teakwood desk just in time to catch a glimpse of a becoming flush staining her cheeks before she looked down. A few framed photographs of her with Michael taken over the years caught his eye.

"There's a chair by the table over there if you want to make yourself comfortable," she said softly, as if she couldn't force the words out any louder.

Glancing around, he spotted the chair and crossed the room to retrieve it. "Not a lot of visitors?" he asked, attempting to lighten the atmosphere.

"No. Just Michael and Jenny."

The table across the long, narrow room was littered with piles of papers and binders. It was pushed against a window looking into the lush gardens of Hyatt House, overflowing with blooms and foliage in the damp July heat. Before turning away, Rhett noted some spreadsheets and graphs with neat, tiny handwriting in the margins. She'd been keeping track of an abundance of details. To do the right thing? Or to find her own ways of taking over?

Or both?

Again, Rhett's unease returned as he set the chair across from her desk and sat down. Usually he had his target pinned and figured out within hours of their meeting. Definitely within a day. His doubts and questions about Trinity were unusual. He certainly didn't enjoy the constant second-guessing. He needed answers. ASAP.

*You know why she's trying to throw you off track,* his inner cynic said. But the rest of him, the part admittedly attracted to her, reminded him to keep an open mind. He liked to think he could do that—it wasn't his fault the people he was brought in to condemn usually proved his inner cynic right.

The inner struggle drove him to his feet once more, and he crossed to the wall of whiteboards. "What made you decide to use this method?" he asked. He told himself that being able to see the data out in the open like this was good for his investigation.

"Michael and I came up with it. I've always been a visually oriented person, and writing things down helps them stick. Typing information into a computer doesn't do the same thing for me, hence the whiteboards. Michael, on the other hand, was more at home with spreadsheets and data-mining programs."

That made sense. "So he knew you pretty well?"

"As you could tell by the photographs, we've known each other a long time."

*Long enough for you to learn his weaknesses?*

"He taught me a lot through the years, about business, art and people. Though very few people want to acknowledge those years we worked together."

"What did you do before you married?" he asked, though he knew the answer already.

"Same thing I do now," Trinity said with the smallest of enchanting smiles. That pinpoint of happiness drew Rhett into her words. "I managed Michael's charity, *Maison de Jardin*. It's a shelter for abused women and children."

"Sounds fulfilling."

"It is." Her smile grew even softer. "And heartbreaking. And satisfying. Michael wholeheartedly believed in the charity and wanted to ensure it continued—despite his aunt and uncle's wishes."

Rhett let that pass, for now.

"Michael and I spent a lot of time together. Not just at the charity." The very fact that she didn't elaborate made Rhett all the more curious. "He tended to process issues and problems out loud. When we were together, he would talk through the ins and outs of business strategies just as much as he spoke about art and movies and travel."

"Sounds boring for you."

"Nothing with Michael was ever boring." The sad shadow that crossed her expression brought an odd tightness to Rhett's chest. "He wasn't just my husband, he was my best friend."

But was he her bedmate once they were married? Rhett wanted to know—even though it wasn't his place to ask.

Or was it? Was she lying about her husband's intentions in marrying her? Or her intentions? After all, other than sex, why would Michael have married a woman much younger than him, so much below his own station in life? Or was Rhett simply blowing the evidence of the unshared bedroom out of proportion? He knew more than anyone how odd the rich and famous could be. And people slept in different rooms for a myriad of reasons…it didn't necessarily mean they hadn't been intimate.

But how would that knowledge affect the court case? If he could get her to confide the true emotional depth of her relationship with her husband… After all, wasn't that what he was here for?

But first, he had to get her to trust him.

As he focused in on her expression once more, Rhett noticed she seemed to be struggling with something just as much as he was—though he hoped his expression wasn't nearly as revealing as hers.

"Look—" she paused to swallow hard "—I know other people must have mentioned that I grew up at *Maison de Jardin*. That is true. I did."

At least she wasn't hiding her roots from him. This part of the story intrigued him more than he wanted it to.

"My mother and I moved there when I was ten after… Well, it doesn't matter. But Michael was very good to us. We came there just before his parents died. He was very lost and spent a lot of time helping at *Maison de Jardin* during that very dark period of his life."

"So it meant a lot to him?"

"It did. More than a lot of people know." She grimaced, seemingly struggling to say something. "I don't want to appear judgmental or—"

"Trinity." He waited until she met his gaze head-on before continuing. "Whatever it is, just tell me."

He really wanted to know. He needed to know. And holding her gaze with his own deepened that need in a way he didn't want to examine.

"Michael's aunt and uncle—there's something you don't understand. Something no one on the board seems to understand. This court case, it has nothing to do with the businesses."

*Wait a minute...* "How so?"

"Oh, in the long run, the income from the businesses might help them. But that's not why they want the inheritance."

Her gaze went to the wall over his shoulder next to the door to the other offices. Rhett turned to find a gorgeous portrait of a house. No, house was an understatement. It was three stories of astonishing Queen Anne brick architecture. It had three chimneys. A turret on the third floor. Arched bay windows on the lower level and a balcony over the front door. It was enormous and in incredible repair despite what must be significant age.

Some houses were portrayed as scary. Some majestic. Some transcendent. Despite the obvious grandeur of the building in the painting, Rhett felt a sense of welcoming, of the promise of protection within its walls. The small nameplate at the bottom confirmed that this was *Maison de Jardin.*

"You see, whoever gains control of Michael's inheritance doesn't just gain his place on the board of Hyatt Heights. They gain full control over the charity."

"There's no board for the charity?" Rhett asked, tiny alarm bells sounding in his brain.

Trinity slowly shook her head. "There are no checks and balances, which means they would be able to do with *Maison de Jardin* whatever they want." Her gaze returned to the painting. "There would be no one to stop them."

"From doing what?" Rhett's voice came out hushed, though they were alone in the room.

"What they've wanted all along...sell *Maison de Jardin* to the highest bidder."

# Five

Trinity paused outside the door to the breakfast room and took a few deep breaths. The faint clink of silverware told her Rhett was already inside. She'd tossed and turned, knowing that he slept just across the hall. The anticipation she felt at seeing him again confirmed she needed to keep him at arm's length.

She'd never been one to be charmed by a handsome face, but she was beginning to wonder about herself. Then again, the understanding and shock he'd exhibited when she'd talked about her in-laws yesterday might have something to do with her curiosity, too.

Sympathetic people had been few and far between in her lifetime, much less since marrying Michael. Since his death, she'd restricted her comments about the Hyatts to private discussions with her lawyer, so she wasn't sure what had prompted her revelation the day before. Some days she simply felt so alone in the task Michael had left for her. Apparently she hadn't been able to resist unburdening herself when Rhett seemed to lend a sympathetic ear.

Still, the last thing she needed was to get too attached. Her life was already complicated enough, and she had too many obligations that other people might not understand.

*So suck it up, buttercup!* Time to go back to standing on her own two feet.

With that little pep talk, she forced herself through the doorway and gave Rhett a cautious smile. "Good morning," she said.

She let herself absorb the atmosphere of one of her favorite places in the house. A double set of French doors, open to the coolness of the morning, allowed in dappled sunshine and the scent of flowers from the luscious gardens outside. She could even hear the buzzing of a bee as it worked the blossoms of the bougainvillea that framed the doorway.

With a quick but deep breath, she turned to the buffet along the opposite wall. Normally the cook who had been with Michael since he'd been a teenager would have prepared a simple breakfast just for Trinity. But the presence of a guest called for a more elaborate, traditionally Southern spread of biscuits, grits, gravy, bacon, sausage and omelets that left the buffet overflowing. It was a little overboard for just two people but the cook missed preparing meals for visitors, who had been frequent when Michael had been alive.

"Have a chance to look over those cash flow concepts last night?" Rhett asked.

The focus on business helped her relax slightly. "Yes. And I've started working on a strategy guide for you and Bill to vet…" She couldn't stop the frown that pulled down her brows. "Although I still feel we should do more to help the employees themselves, rather than focusing solely on creating profits."

"You can—by ensuring them a stable and profitable business that guarantees jobs and income."

His matter-of-fact tone was understandable but frustrating. "But the business would be nothing without its employees. Shouldn't we reassure them we're concerned about their welfare?" That would take more than words. She knew. She'd been there.

"I understand your concern, but it's idealistic," he said as he lowered his plate onto the small table next to a window overlooking the patio. The mounds of omelet, bacon and biscuits barely made a dent in the offerings, but Rhett looked happy. "Right now, we need to ensure the business is the strongest it can be."

"Actually, a focus on employees was something Michael felt very strongly about." Her appetite shriveled as she thought about betraying his legacy. Still, she spooned a small portion of scrambled eggs and a biscuit onto her plate. "Employee benefits and policies was something he and his uncle continually disagreed on."

"He sounds like a good guy."

Why had Rhett's voice suddenly hardened? Trinity glanced over but his expression was neutral. "You don't believe me?" she asked. "Michael knew how to be tough when he needed to be."

"And now is one of those times," he said, Rhett's voice softening as he watched her. "I'm not saying take advantage or short the employees in any way. I'm just saying the focus has to be on the bigger picture. For now. The kindhearted rarely survive long in big business. With these companies on shaky ground, you need to remember that. Be tough."

He was right. This was something she could not fail at, so taking Rhett's advice was essential. There was too much at stake. "I guess my own experience is with an organization like *Maison de Jardin* that's less focused on profit and more focused on people. I know that, but it's still hard to get away from."

When he didn't respond, she glanced over at him to find him watching her with a little more intensity than before. He chewed slowly, looking deep in thought. She felt the urge to squirm but calmed herself by pouring a cup of her favorite chicory coffee and taking a sip.

From behind her, he said, "I understand that. You've done a good job there, I'm sure. The skills are transferable, but the focus is just different."

His words nagged at her as she crossed to her seat and set her plate on the table. She couldn't stop herself from asking, "Are you always tough?" She bit her lip as she sat down, but couldn't hold the next question inside. "Is it always about the bottom line for you?"

If she hadn't been watching him, she would have missed his reaction. Because it wasn't the words he spoke, or rather, didn't speak. It was his face.

It was as if his expression cracked, whether from surprise or irritation or something else, she wasn't sure. But almost immediately she recognized that she was seeing Rhett's true self, one he rarely—if ever—let anyone see. His gray eyes went wide. She saw a mixture of shock and pain there that both saddened and intrigued her. She leaned forward before he was able to lock himself down tight.

She opened her mouth to ask more, propelled by some internal need for answers, but her phone rang. They both started at the sound. It took her a moment to pull her gaze away from his face to focus on the noise. Bill's name scrolled across the screen.

She connected the call but had to clear her throat before any words would come out. "Yes?"

She only caught a few rushed words, but her brain refused to comprehend them. "I'm sorry. What?"

"There's been another post. You might want to take a look." He paused a moment before going on, "I'm sorry, Trinity."

She barely acknowledged his words as she hung up. She was too busy trying to access the site on her phone. Dread settled hard in her stomach. Why was this person tormenting her like this?

Sure enough, the new post was all about her. This blogger didn't play around. There were already dozens of comments. But it was the picture that held Trinity captivated, cutting off her breath for long moments.

The post consisted of two photos side by side. The one on the left was a picture of a picture. Someone had obviously gotten their hands on the old photograph—

one she knew was framed here in the house. Her at fifteen, all awkward smile and hand-me-down clothes. A twenty-five-year-old Michael stood by her side, dapper in his dress shirt and tie. They stood outside *Maison de Jardin*, comfortable in their friendship, even at that age.

The second picture featured her now, dressed to the nines in the sapphire gown she'd worn to the museum event because Michael had picked it out for her. Then and now. Poor and rich. Awkward and soberly mourning, though no one else would believe it. Certainly no one who had commented had taken that view.

And then the hateful caption:

Planning ahead? Guess she got what she worked all those years for.

Trinity's throat closed up.

She could remember the very moment the first photograph had been taken. The happiness she'd felt having her best friend by her side. Having his acceptance of her as something like a sister, despite the differences of age and wealth between them.

To have it used against her in this comparison post was vaguely ironic in a way she couldn't fully grasp through the hurt of the accusation. She forced herself to take a shallow breath.

Of course, people thought that. They had to. But the only ones to ever say it out loud were Patricia and Richard. To see it on the screen for anyone to see…

Suddenly she felt a warm hand at the nape of her

neck, right over the tense knot developing there. The tightness melted immediately.

She wanted to dive into that warmth, to hide in a cocoon where no one could find her. Just as her eyes drifted closed, she remembered.

This was Rhett. He couldn't be trusted. After what she'd just seen, such personal ammunition that could have been taken from this very house, she was beginning to think no one could.

So she forced the starch back into her spine and subtly pulled away. For long moments, he lingered by her side, his close presence both calling to her and inciting fear. Finally, unable to stand it any longer, she looked up to see him staring at the screen of her phone.

Part of her shriveled up inside to have him see it, to expose him to the rumors about her, even though someone had probably told him before now.

"Started gold digging at a young age, huh?"

Rhett could sense the stiffening of Trinity's muscles, her defenses rising against the accusing eyes of the world.

Usually he would never have been that crude but he had a growing need to get some real insight into Trinity's intentions. Good or bad, he simply needed to know.

Though he'd only meant to be flippant, Trinity's face spasmed in pain, leaving him with an uncomfortable feeling. One that wasn't familiar. It took a few seconds before he realized he was contrite.

"Where do they get this stuff?" he scoffed, surprising himself as he attempted to take the pressure off.

That shouldn't be his mode of operation. He should be pressing harder, not consoling her, but he couldn't seem to help himself.

"People only see what they're looking for," he continued.

He'd said the words time and again to his partner. It was his way of explaining why people could fool others over and over and get away with it. The truth was in the eye of the beholder.

He couldn't stop his gentle squeeze of her neck, but then he made himself let go and step away.

But the urge to touch her again wouldn't subside. The feel of her warm, silken skin lingered against his palm. Instead he focused on what he'd just said. Were his comforting words only an attempt to get into her good graces? Or was her vulnerability getting to him?

Finally, she turned those oh-so-soulful eyes away from him. Only then could he focus once more on the pictures still displayed on her phone.

In the first photograph, Trinity looked so innocent that it almost hurt. So young. So eager. So ripe for the picking. Her expression seemed to hold an awareness that Michael's friendship wasn't normal for someone in her situation. Had Michael taken the opportunity to make her more than a friend at some point before their marriage? Surely, he had in all those years that they'd known each other.

Then why had he suddenly married her when he did?

In the photo, Michael exuded confidence and knowledge of his place in the world. And a comfortable sense of belonging at Trinity's side that Rhett was suddenly jealous of, even though they weren't touching. Why had someone ten years Trinity's senior felt the need to befriend one of the children in his care?

That's when Rhett spotted something that made him double back. He leaned in, unsure if it was a trick of the light. The photo was grainy, obviously a picture of a picture. But was that an angry, raised scar snaking along Trinity's hairline?

Slowly he reached out to rub the tip of his finger over her cheek in the picture. "What's this?" he asked.

The jolt of her body told him he'd gone too far, but he wouldn't back down. And he didn't pull away from her. He couldn't tell if he was staying so close to put on the pressure or to savor the feel of her. When he didn't move, she finally spoke.

"People have made up my story to suit themselves my entire life," she said, skirting his direct question. Her voice was shaky at first, but grew steadier with each word. "Guess it's more interesting than the boring truth."

"I doubt anything about you is boring," he countered. It was meant to charm her but he realized it was true.

The scar fascinated him. It was red and raised but still partially hidden by her hair in the picture. A quick glance showed no evidence of scarring at her now-smooth temple. Had the injury been less severe than it appeared in the photo?

As if she knew he was looking, Trinity turned to gaze out the bay window of the breakfast nook.

"You didn't answer my question."

Trinity was instantly on her feet, her chair skittering

back a few inches on the polished wood floor. "It was an accident," she said, her voice clipped.

Her movements were tight as she crossed the room, stalking over the tile floor until she could press her palms down against the smooth wood of the buffet. Instinct told him she wasn't surveying the food for a second helping. She wanted away from him, but she hadn't left the room.

Why?

He couldn't stop himself. As if his body had a mind of its own, he followed her, stepping closer than he knew she would be comfortable with. Watching her. Needing that reaction on some gut level.

"What kind of accident?"

The sudden anger that vibrated off her surprised him...and intrigued him even more.

"Why should I tell you anything?" she finally barked. "So you can use it against me like everyone else?"

He wanted to refute her words, be angry that she would assume such a thing. But the truth was, his assignment was to do exactly that.

"Why would you assume I want to hurt you?" he asked instead, his voice low and quiet.

Her face suddenly scrunched up in confusion. "I don't know, I just—" She shook her head as if to clear her thoughts away. "You wouldn't understand."

"Try me."

There was no denying his need to touch her. He took another step closer, reaching his hand around until he could cup her chin. Turning her face to his woke the urge to kiss her, but he held himself back. Barely. Her answer was more important to him.

"Tell me, Trinity."

"Why should I?"

She backed away, giving him a better view of her face and the protective curve of her arms around her waist. Still he kept his connection with her, skin to skin.

"Because I need to know." The words came out of nowhere and were the most honest thing he'd ever told a target. Nerves exploded in his gut for the first time in a long time. A target. He didn't want to think about her that way…ever.

She shook her head slightly. "I don't think you'd understand. Most people don't." She swallowed, drawing his gaze down to the smooth column of her throat. How vulnerable. How tempting. "Very few people understand what it's like to live under such hostile scrutiny. Everywhere I turn, someone is waiting to twist the truth to suit their own devices. I've lived in this fishbowl for weeks. Have you?" Her voice hardened. "Can you even begin to understand what it's like to not be able to trust anyone anymore?"

Rhett felt his eyelids fall to half-mast. His gaze dropped from her soulful brown eyes to the pale skin he stroked with his thumb. Despite his resistance, his mind took him back to another time. The defining moments that taught him the very lesson that had changed his path forever. Hardened him. Broken him.

"Oh, yes, I understand," he murmured.

Though the back of his mind was screaming at him to shut up, he couldn't keep the words inside. On some level, he owed them to her for his many deceptions. "I know all about being scrutinized and used. Women aren't the only ones vulnerable to that treatment."

"What happened?" she asked, her soft voice barely registering over the memories flooding his brain.

He felt his mouth twist, knowing he was revealing the true amount of cynicism in his heart. It was an emotion he normally kept deeply buried beneath a charming facade. "I trusted the wrong person. I thought I was in love, only to find out she simply wanted me for my money."

# Six

Trinity's anger melted immediately, leaving behind an uncomfortable mixture of awareness and sympathy for the man standing so close to her. The heat from his body drew her. Made her want to sway closer until he gathered her into his strong arms and protected her from the prying eyes of the world.

But no. She'd learned early to stand on her own two feet. Protection was a fairy tale even Michael hadn't been able to provide.

Rhett's expression betrayed his surprise and regret over what he'd said. Given her own reluctance to share, she couldn't blame him. It must be even harder for men to reveal that they'd been blindsided like that.

"I'm sorry, Rhett," her sympathy compelled her to say. Maybe he was something of a kindred spirit.

He stepped away from her. "I'm not."

That was definitely surprising. "Why?"

"It taught me a lot." Though the words were confident, steady, Rhett's smile was strained. "It put me on the path I'm on today. There's no sense regretting it."

*But are you happy that it happened?* She couldn't speak the words, even though they resounded in her head. As hard as it had been since his death, she would never have given up her friendship with Michael for anything. Could never regret accepting his marriage request...even though it had led to some of the most deeply unhappy times of her life. She hadn't known the scrutiny and backlash she would face.

Or how much of her life would be exposed. She'd learned from a young age to keep to herself. Then growing up in a group home, where everyone seemed to be in everyone else's business, she'd become very private. So much so, she'd rather keep hidden or just not talk. Being thrust into the public eye was more devastating than she was willing to let on.

As if he'd read her mind, Rhett said, "Enough of my sordid history. So what happened? Fell off your bike? Got hit in a sport?"

Trinity wished it had been any number of mundane childhood accidents. Ones easily explained away. But she hadn't spoken of the incident since it happened. Luckily the scar had long ago moved up under her thick hairline, covering the source of so many questions she'd had to brush off in her early teens.

She'd never even spoken of it with Michael. Though he hadn't had to ask the details. He'd learned them from her devastated mother while Trinity had been hospitalized after the brutal beating her father had given her.

"Car accident?"

Rhett's expression had grown more somber, showing a concern she hadn't expected.

"Tell me it was a car accident and not—"

"We didn't own a car."

He blanched, and his reaction struck a chord in her. Which prompted her to tell the story she hadn't told a soul in her life.

"We met Michael at Children's Hospital. Mama and me." She swallowed, wrapping her arms around her stomach. "He had walked over after visiting his father, who was in an adjacent hospital after a car accident that proved fatal, and found my mother crying in the emergency room lobby. Alone."

She tried to cover the rest of the story as straightforwardly as possible. "My father had slammed me against the fireplace, cutting my face open from temple to ear. Mama didn't know what to do. Even though he'd been abusive before, we stayed because there was no place to go. But this was the worst he'd ever hurt me."

Trinity swallowed hard. Why, after all these years, did this memory make her throat tighten? It wasn't like she cared about her father. He'd been cut from her life that very night.

Michael had made that possible.

"She took me to the hospital. We had no money, nothing from home. Just the clothes on our back. We knew we wouldn't be able to return without serious repercussions. Michael—he took care of everything."

He'd paid her hospital bill in cash. Had overlooked their lack of possessions and money and driven them to *Maison de Jardin* as soon as Trinity was released. Sent a couple of huge guys to their house to get their clothes. It was the first big step he'd taken to help another person *in person*, as opposed to just writing a check, and it had made as big an impact on him as it had on Trinity. Especially since his dad had been dying in a nearby hospital bed.

"How old were you?" Rhett asked, his quiet voice breaking her out of her reverie.

"I was ten," she said. "Michael was twenty."

He'd taken a special interest in her from that moment on. Never romantic. Despite the differences in their upbringings and social status, they'd eventually become inseparable. He'd helped her get her degree, and she'd formally gone to work for him while she was at university. Informally, she and her mother had been helping run the charity for years.

The wound that started it all was hidden now, just like her story had been. She felt a twinge of regret. Would Rhett think less of her for it? Lord knew there were many through the years who had looked down on her for living on charity most of her life. Her mother, too. But they'd never stopped giving back—both to *Maison de Jardin* and to the other women and children who had passed through the home over the years. Michael had relied on them, and they'd repaid him with everything they had.

Even to the point of marriage…

Trinity lifted her chin. Regardless of Rhett's reaction, she knew she'd made the right choices in her life. "*Maison* is a godsend to women like my mother and me. It must continue. Those lives are worth way more than the cost of some land."

Silence reigned in the cozy room for long minutes, leaving Trinity acutely aware that the two of them were alone with each other. The air felt thick with revelation. She wasn't sure where to look or what to say next.

At long last she dragged her gaze from the gardens outside to look into Rhett's eyes. Where she'd expected to find judgment, she instead saw an intensity that penetrated any barriers she might put up between them. She'd already felt raw. Now she was bare.

"You're very right, Trinity," he finally said.

No words of trite sympathy. Just a simple acknowledgment. Her body relaxed. She drew in a deep breath. "Would you like to see it?"

He was more than likely working for the enemy. The best she knew to do was to lure him over to her side. To help him see the good in *Maison de Jardin* and the women and children there.

But part of her request was personal. For the first time, she needed to share a part of her life that very few had seen.

He tilted his head to the side and silently regarded her. What was she doing? Was the risk worth it?

She wasn't even sure if she was relieved when he said, "I believe I would."

"You're going soft, man."

Rhett scoffed at his partner's words later that night

while ignoring the twinge of guilt they kicked up. "I just think this is important."

"Whether your clients are telling the truth or not isn't important."

"Since when?" Had they really come to that point?

Chris was silent for a minute. "Maybe that's the wrong way to put it. Yes, we want to do the right thing. But when was the last time a client was wrong?"

Never. Rhett didn't want to admit it, because it would undermine his position, but he knew where Chris was coming from. "I just think there's more at stake here than a simple inheritance."

On the surface, the charity seemed like nothing compared to the overall worth of Michael's estate. Why would the Hyatts dismantle it? Was Trinity right? Were they looking for fast cash?

Besides, the charity Michael had started seemed to do a lot of good. He remembered Trinity's story. Were the Hyatts actually heartless enough to do away with all that? "What if these people are looking to get their hands on the building and land just to sell it quick?"

"Then that's their prerogative. But if you're worried about it, don't you need more evidence than just the word of the woman you're there to investigate?"

True. Rhett rubbed his hand over his face. Was he losing his edge? He tried to tell himself this was about protecting a home for abused women and children—the very one he would visit tomorrow. So why did he keep seeing soft brown eyes that begged him to look deeper?

"Just look into it from your end," he barked.

"All right. Though I think it's crazy."

Shaking his head, Rhett quickly concluded his call with Chris but couldn't stop the pacing. He needed to find out more about both *Maison de Jardin* and Michael's aunt and uncle. Questioning Trinity was an option, but could he trust the answers he would be given? He wanted to, but having Chris dig deeper was a better way to go. And he needed to stay objective, no matter what.

He paused inside the door to his bedroom, knowing what he had to do. It wasn't like he hadn't searched for information in a house before in the dead of night.

This was no different.

Hell, it should be a lot easier, since Trinity and he were alone in this portion of the house…right next to the wing that held the offices.

Having made his decision, he wasted no time, utilizing stealth and speed as he made his way to the lower floor. He might find nothing. They might keep the office suite locked. He might encounter someone along the way. Cleaning staff. The butler. He'd just have to see.

He passed the door to the little office they'd given him, using only the flashlight on his phone to show him the way. The door to the other offices was almost directly across the hall. The knob turned easily beneath his palm.

*She is too trusting.*

He wasn't as lucky inside. Without turning on the lights, he tried the tall filing cabinets along one wall of Michael's office. They were all locked. The computer was password protected. The cabinet on the hutch above the desk was also locked. He glanced toward the secretary's office. Maybe he should check there?

His heartbeat remained steady. Hands sure. But his mind raced, running through the options that might be open to him.

What he hoped to find, he wasn't sure. But he needed more facts than what he had. Facts, not conjectures. Or at the very least, clues as to what Michael Hyatt had been thinking. Who else would know his family and all their secrets?

He stood, uncertain for a moment. *Think…think…*

As if by divine guidance, the light from his phone caught the edge of something under the desk he hadn't noticed before. Bending down, he realized the desk had a hanging drawer. Even as he reached for it, Rhett knew it wouldn't be locked. Something just told him this one had been overlooked.

Sure enough, the drawer slid soundlessly open.

There was a small crush of tabs to peruse. Rhett quickly realized why this drawer was probably open. It held all of Michael's personal files—Trinity and her secretary were probably accessing them a lot dealing with the legalities of Michael's death. Health insurance. A surprisingly large medical file. Household bills. Original documents. All things Rhett found himself uncomfortably curious about.

And there it was, all the way in the back.

Background Investigations

A quick glance at the top page looked like a financial accounting…and not a good one. Richard's name appeared a time or two. Definitely a file Rhett needed to take a look at. The next one back looked just as intriguing. *Maison de Jardin*.

The folder was slim, which probably meant it held something innocuous like deeds and insurance documents. Not much more. Still, it wouldn't hurt for him to borrow them both for a few hours.

Carefully he made sure the drawer was firmly shut, then crossed toward the door. He was only halfway there when the light from the hallway blinked on, creating a bright line beneath the door.

Someone was coming.

His heart rate picked up. He rushed back to the desk and dropped the folders beneath it. No time to put them away. He hurried back toward the door, so that he grabbed the handle at the same time as the person outside. But he kept plowing forward, his alibi forming in his mind already.

Then he made contact with soft curves in all the right places.

Instantly his body went on high alert…but not because of fear or nerves. Holding this woman evoked pure adrenaline. Something he'd never experienced before. He couldn't fight it. Didn't want to. He could only enjoy the rush.

"Trinity," he groaned.

Her muscles were taut, as though she were preparing to pull away from whomever she'd run into. Blinded by the light from the hallway, Rhett had only touch to rely upon. He felt her relax, her body melt into his. He leaned into the sensation, supporting her weight as his mouth came down on hers.

Her lips were pliant, almost as if she were expecting this. And he couldn't wait any longer. He pressed into her from lips to knees, desperate to imprint her body with his. Her curves felt so right. She was no longer the elegant representation of a lady by day, but instead the full impression of a true woman by night. A woman who needed him, if the way she clutched his biceps meant anything.

He lost himself in the exploration of her lips, tracing the seam with the tip of his tongue until she opened for him. She was sweet without sugar and left him aching for more. Her taste, her response seemed to have been made solely for him. She moaned low in her throat, sending a thrill down his spine.

He knew kissing her was wrong. But right now, it felt oh so right. Nothing would make him walk away… not even a pesky thing like logic.

Once more her fingers dug into his upper arms, her body pressing closer. He let his hand slide down the curve of her spine to lock her against him. The throb of his body made him moan. He was forced to pull away to gasp for air.

"Trinity," he muttered, his voice turned guttural in his need. "I want you so badly."

In an instant her body froze. All that precious molten movement shuttered to a stop. Hands that had clutched at him now pushed him away, demanding release. He could do nothing but obey.

"I'm sorry," she gasped, backing away one step, then another. "I'm sorry. I just can't do this."

Then she spun on her heel and disappeared into the light.

# Seven

The next morning, Trinity paused at the top of the stairs as her stomach cramped. She panted through the sensation. There wasn't much else she could do.

After all, meeting Rhett this morning wasn't optional. It was an obligation. A necessity.

She'd wanted to show him *Maison de Jardin*, especially after their discussion yesterday. If she could get someone of his stature to see the value of the charity, she might have an ally, and she could sorely use one. But after last night, they needed to have a very uncomfortable conversation.

Only after her humiliating flight back to her room last night had the questions come. She'd been so startled by his presence, and then his kiss, that she hadn't properly questioned why he'd been in Michael's office to begin with. How could that not have been her highest priority?

The urge to laugh and cry at the same time almost overwhelmed her. If only he knew. She'd been so far out of her league last night…but no one would believe her if she told them. Just the memory of Rhett's kiss was enough to evoke shivers.

That was the last thing she needed to be thinking about right now. She forced herself down the steps one at a time, a deliberate pace even though this was the last place she wanted to be and Rhett was the last person she wanted to face.

Her brain refused to rehearse the questions she needed to ask. Instead her attention was caught by Rhett's appearance through the side doorway. He came to a stop at the bottom of the stairs.

Trinity tightened her grip on the banister. It wouldn't do to fall just because this man threw her off.

His expression was somber this morning, just as she imagined hers was. She tried to lighten the mood with a slight smile, though she probably failed. Mornings after weren't something she knew how to deal with. And he wasn't giving her any visual clues on how to proceed.

Luckily her driver, Roberto, came through the front door just as she reached the bottom of the stairs. A blessing of a distraction.

"Everything is packed and ready, ma'am," he said in his slightly accented voice.

Trinity calmed…for the moment, at least.

"Thank you, Roberto." She cast a quick glance toward Rhett. "Shall we?"

She didn't even wait long enough to catch his nod. Instead she strode across the foyer with a confidence she was far from feeling. She heard his footsteps behind her.

Of course, she was simply walking into a trap of her own making. Roberto held the door for them to enter the back of the Bentley, and then she was confined for the next thirty minutes with the very man she'd been kissing last night.

Why did her brain keep reminding her of that? How exciting it had felt to have his arms around her. How the sexy scent of him had filled her senses. How her body had leaped to life at his touch.

*Stop it!*

Rhett didn't have the same reservations about bringing up what happened as she did.

"Trinity, I'm sorry about—"

"Why were you in Michael's office last night?"

It was the only way she could come up with to cut him off at the pass.

"I apologize, Trinity. I should have explained myself last night, but then we…"

He just couldn't keep from mentioning it, could he? Her face burned and she turned to look out the window.

"I didn't turn on the lights when I went downstairs last night because I didn't want to disturb anyone. In the light from my flashlight, I took a wrong turn. The door wasn't locked, so—"

"I'll have to talk to Jenny about that."

She sounded super prim. Wow, she really was turning into an old maid. Still, they had to be more careful.

Even though she knew everything in the offices was secured, that didn't mean they needed to leave the door unlocked with a guest in the house. Jenny had been the last one out the night before.

"I had just realized my mistake and was heading back out when I...ran into you."

Suddenly she felt his hand rest lightly on her arm. As much as she wished she could continue to avoid his gaze, that touch compelled her to turn around to face him. Still, she couldn't drag her eyes up to meet his, but instead stared intently at the smooth gray fabric of his polo.

"I am very sorry about last night," he said. "Everything about it was unexpected, but—"

Out of the corner of her eye, she caught sight of his hand going up to run through the silvery strands that stood out against dark hair. She couldn't help but let her gaze follow. Why did he have to be so handsome? Why did he have to seem intelligent and helpful? Why did he have to be affiliated with *them*?

Her heart pounded as she remembered the feel of his lips moving over hers. So powerful. So commanding. She'd wanted nothing more than to surrender.

But she didn't trust herself to make good judgments right now. Michael was the only man she'd ever trusted. And when it came to romance—if that was even something Rhett was interested in—she was the last person who would know what to ask.

No, it was safer right now to focus on the chaos already in her life, rather than inviting more.

"But what we shared last night—"

"Please don't."

Thankfully, her harsh whisper silenced any words that might be far too tempting for her.

"Even if I wasn't a widow of only six short weeks—" she swallowed hard, forcing herself not to reveal the truth that would make his judgment even more harsh "—I simply can't get involved right now. It's just too much."

She waited for him to offer an excuse or argue. Instead he watched her in enigmatic silence for a few moments before he said, "I understand."

He didn't seem to be judging, but she couldn't help but notice that he backed down quickly. And didn't that make her a hypocrite? She didn't want any romantic complications in her life, but her ego would have appreciated him arguing a little harder for them.

She turned back toward the window, hoping to hide her confusion. What the heck was wrong with her?

Thankfully they were turning onto the *Maison de Jardin* estate. It wasn't huge in terms of land. Over the years, all estates in the Garden District had shrunk as the city encroached on them. But the house…that was another story.

As soon as the car stopped in the front drive, Trinity was out the door; she didn't wait for Roberto to come around and open it for her. She paused in the drive, taking a moment to breathe in the smell of hyacinth and roses. Her gaze roamed over the outside of the mansion. Every time she returned here, that stone facade greeted her, welcoming her home. And yet she always saw it with fresh eyes, no matter how many years she'd lived here.

"How long has the house been here?" Rhett asked from the other side of the Bentley.

"It was built in the 1870s, I believe," Trinity said. "James Hyatt brought big shipping to New Orleans with luxury liners he operated all over the world. He wanted nothing more than to have a large family, but every generation seems to have only birthed one son."

"This is breathtaking," Rhett said, his gaze roaming over the ornamental brick and the landscaped grounds.

"The inside is even more fascinating," Trinity assured him. "When James built the house for his first bride, he spared no expense. The idea was to create a legacy that endured. The fact that she never had children was the deepest sorrow of her life, according to her journals."

She turned to smile at him. "I can only hope the purpose Michael and his parents put the house to has made her happy."

He didn't scoff or brush off her sentimentality. "I'm sure it has."

"His second wife was able to give birth to a son, the only child of that generation."

As she stepped around the car toward the front door, Rhett's hand closed around her arm right above the elbow. She glanced back at him in surprise, unable to suppress the jolt of awareness that came from the contact. If she'd hoped that her reaction to his touch the night before had been a product of the night and her own isolation, she'd been fooling herself.

He must have felt it, too, because he immediately let go, pulling back and spreading his fingers in a gesture that said *I come in peace*. His tongue swept out over his lips. Did his mouth go as dry as hers? Was his brief glance down to her lips a hint that he wanted to kiss her as much as she wanted him to?

Even though she'd told him no.

"Trinity," he finally said, "I just want you to know… I see your point."

She tilted her head to the side. "What point?" Her heart pounded; she was anxious to hear his next words.

He gestured to the house and sculpted grounds. "About the house. I don't know what the whole story is, but I can see that this property would be very valuable to someone who wanted to off-load it."

His gaze was assessing, seeing the worth of what was in front of him like a true businessman. But she found herself hoping he could see even more than just dollars and land values. Would he see the worth of the people who called *Maison de Jardin* home?

If he could, she just might have an ally after all.

Rhett may have been impressed with the outer trappings of *Maison de Jardin*, but the inside was awe-inspiring. The fact that the Hyatts could have bought any house in Louisiana to make the base of their safe house for battered women and children, but chose to place it on the original family estate, spoke to the quality of people they were.

People who didn't do anything halfway.

"Rhett Brannon, this is Madison. She's my replacement as director here at *Maison de Jardin*."

Madison had flaming auburn hair, pale skin and freckles. She appeared strong despite her less-than-average height and was dressed practically in jeans and a T-shirt.

Rhett glanced over at Trinity as she and the other woman shared soft smiles. Did Trinity's hold a hint of sadness? Had she truly found her calling, like her mother, in running *Maison de Jardin*? Or had she seen it as an opportunity to better herself?

Despite the Hyatts' poisonous description of Trinity, he was leaning toward the latter explanation. Her motives seemed pure. It left him a little stunned that he was ready to admit this to himself about a target for the first time in his entire career.

Then he realized the women were watching him expectantly. He must have missed something. "I'm sorry?"

"Would you like a tour?" Trinity asked.

"Oh, of course."

Rhett noticed a few women watching from the doorway of another room down the hall, and how they retreated as Madison led them that way. They entered an impressive two-story library, but Rhett had a hard time focusing on the incredible book collection. The three women were now watching him warily from near the fireplace, their expressions ranging from subtle defiance to wide-eyed fear. He almost closed his eyes as he realized the source, but reminded himself they didn't get the luxury of turning away from what had happened to them.

Instead he nodded with as much respect as he knew

how to show with a silent gesture, and kept his distance so that he didn't spark any sense of threat.

Still, their expressions lingered in his mind as Trinity and Madison led him through halls and rooms filled with warmth. Dark shiny woods were everywhere. Fireplaces for the rare winterish night in the bayou. Intriguing nooks and crannies that he could just imagine young women like Trinity using to curl up with a good book. And there were enough creaks and groans to elicit a friendly ghost story or two.

"This is the floor Michael's parents had made into suites," Madison explained as they came to the third-floor landing. "It houses women with small children so they can all stay together, as opposed to the single women and teenagers in the individual rooms on the second floor."

Suddenly a door opened and a tiny figure in black ran down the hall to slam into Trinity's legs. Rhett automatically reached out to steady her, but she braced herself pretty well. She barely swayed as the munchkin called out her name. But it was the soft smile easing her expression that enchanted him.

She knelt down next to what Rhett realized was a toddler in a costume, just as a woman came out of the same door. "Barrett," she called. "Come back here."

The little boy twisted around with a serious expression on his light brown face. "Not Barrett, Mama," he said, making his annoyance plain despite the half mask he wore. "I'm Batman."

Rhett pressed his lips together to keep his laughter inside, noticing that Trinity and Madison did the same.

Batman's mama was not as amused. "No, you're Barrett. And you could hurt Miss Trinity doing that."

"It's okay," Trinity said. She smiled down at the young man. "Did you want to show me your costume?"

"I'm Batman."

"I see. And a very handsome Batman you are."

"I'm a superhero."

"Do superheroes like cookies?" Madison asked, garnering the toddler's full attention. "Because I believe Roberto just unloaded some cookies that Miss Marie might not have put away yet."

Barrett rushed for the stairs, his mother in full sprint behind him. "This kid!" she exclaimed as she rushed past.

Madison and Trinity giggled. "Poor Sofia has had her hands full from day one with that one," Trinity explained.

"I can tell."

"I do need to check that Sofia got herself registered for her radiology tech classes," Trinity said. "Madison, why don't you show Rhett the big surprise downstairs?"

Rhett watched her go, then followed Madison down the opposite hallway. He felt oddly cold without Trinity's running commentary on *Maison de Jardin*. Madison did her best to keep up the history lessons until they came to a set of ornately framed glass doors. "This is the solarium," Madison said as she let him through.

Rhett's eyes grew wide as he took in what was essentially a two-story greenhouse. Fans circulated the warm air.

"Mrs. Hyatt, Michael Hyatt's grandmother, had it

added on to the original house and planted during their first decade of marriage. She did love her gardens."

"If the gardens at Hyatt House hadn't convinced me, this certainly would have."

"She also wanted an 'outdoor area' that the children could enjoy, regardless of the weather. It maintains a steady temperature, and thanks to careful choice of materials, we haven't lost a single pane of glass despite numerous hurricanes in the intervening years."

Incredible. The brick-and-glass structure was home to numerous Japanese maple trees, climbing roses in shades of pink, cream and red, and some kind of pink flowering tree Rhett wasn't familiar with.

He managed to drag his attention away from the fascinating scenery back to the woman with him. Reminding himself that he needed all the information he could get for his job, he asked, "How long have you worked here?"

She looked not quite as old as Trinity, maybe mid to late twenties, with the same haunted shadows in her eyes and determination in her attitude.

"I started helping out a couple of years back." She nodded toward a thick patch of trees and bushes. "My family estate is over there. But I only went on salary last year after my father died. I learned the ropes from Trinity and her mother. As a lifelong caregiver, I felt I had a lot to offer. And Trinity really needed help after her mother passed away."

"How did she pass?"

"A heart attack. Very sudden and sad. We all lost something precious that day." She glanced around the solarium. "I just hope we don't lose everything now... without Mr. Hyatt to protect us."

"Do *you* think a sale is a possibility?" After seeing the place, Rhett could certainly see how anyone would view *Maison de Jardin* as a cash cow.

She involuntarily scoffed, then quickly put her hand over her mouth to conceal it. "Well," she said after clearing her throat, "the last six years I've been here, the current Hyatts have never set foot in *Maison de Jardin*." She shrugged, shaking her head. "I hate to see it end, but thanks to Trinity, we at least have a contingency plan."

That wasn't something Trinity had mentioned to him. "What do you mean?"

Madison didn't seem put off by the question. "I'm not surprised she hasn't said anything. Trinity tends to keep to herself, especially when it's something that might make her look good."

With a glance over her shoulder to make sure her boss wasn't around, she said, "As soon as Mr. Hyatt passed, we had a meeting. She promoted me and said she was essentially stepping down as director. But what that really meant was that she still does just as much work, only she doesn't get paid for it."

"What do you mean?"

"The salary she would have been paid is now used to buy clothes and stockpile food for the families currently living here. She's setting up educational trusts for the women and children we help, even some who have moved out." Madison squeezed her eyes shut, then blinked away the moisture that had filled them. "If the

Hyatts win their lawsuit, she wants everyone set before any sale happens."

Rhett stared over the young woman's head at the black iron scrollwork around the door. His blood pounded in his temples. The evidence was right in front of him. Who did he want to believe?

"That's incredible," he said, speaking more to himself than Madison.

Her smile was big and broad this time. "No, that's Trinity."

# Eight

"**M**adison says you're still paying for some of the women's education even though they've moved on from the house."

Trinity glanced up from the salad she'd been picking at, realizing that she hadn't been tracking the conversation. Going to *Maison de Jardin* was just as upsetting these days as it was inspiring, with all the worry about the future and the burden of keeping everyone safe placed squarely on her shoulders. It was all exhausting. Far too much for her to enjoy lunch at her favorite French Quarter café, located in one of the historic hotels. But feeding Rhett seemed like the proper thing to do.

"I'm sorry. I guess I didn't get the chance to finish talking to you about what we try to do. But yes, some of them get scholarships to continue their education even after their time with us. It just depends on their needs and our ability to meet them."

"How do you know you aren't being taken advantage of?"

She paused to stare at him, her fork halfway to her lips, but he didn't back down. "You know it happens with a lot of charities," he said.

She did. "Yes, and I'm not trying to say it hasn't happened to us. But I'm not naive, nor that trusting. Michael did have some safeguards in place. For instance, all payments go directly to the school and GPA criteria must be met, whether it's a trade school or four-year degree. Stuff like that." She chewed the bite of salad, then wiped her mouth. "Look, I'm not saying the charity is perfect. But it does so much good. I'd hate for it to end because of greed."

The thought of that beautiful building being handed over to two people who couldn't care less about it lingered in her mind like a bad penny. Trinity had always known *Maison de Jardin* was worth a lot of money, given the fact that it was in a prime location on the outskirts of New Orleans' Garden District. But it had been her home, and continued to be the home of so many women and children who desperately needed it.

"You don't think they would offer to simply move the charity somewhere else?"

"Oh, I'm sure they would, because that would make them look like they're doing the right thing." She threw down her napkin with more force than necessary. "How long would that last once the cameras were turned off? Besides, would they offer the same level of help we do now?" She shook her head. "Even if they didn't mine the coffers immediately, I'm convinced Patricia and Richard would slowly steal away every educational fund, clothes fund and food fund until there was nothing left…then probably blame the missing money on mismanagement."

He took a healthy swallow of his Sazerac with cognac, a drink this hotel was famous for. Then he stared down into the elegantly cut crystal glass for a moment before he said, "Well, you're definitely convinced that nothing good will come of this court case. Otherwise you wouldn't have given up your salary like you did."

Startled, Trinity simply stared at him for a moment. Then the truth dawned on her. "I guess Madison told you?"

His expression said *you got me*, but he didn't look the least bit repentant to have been discussing something so personal behind her back. "She did. I'm sure she told me a lot of things you would rather keep under wraps." He leaned forward, meeting her gaze with an intensity that made her uncomfortable. "This isn't a safe course of action, you know."

"I will not let those women be left out in the cold." Trinity tightened her grip on her fork, only realizing she was doing it when the cool handle bit into her fingers. "Besides, I'm not giving up yet. All this worry might be for nothing. I'll be well taken care of once the courts decide in my favor."

But she wasn't fool enough to think winning against the Hyatts would be easy. They were more than willing to play dirty. To be honest, she had to wonder if that blogger was working for them. Still, she believed she wasn't fighting a losing battle.

She had to believe in Michael's plan.

"We've built a family," she insisted, even knowing she sounded more emotional than a businessman probably cared to hear. "These women continue to reach out to each other, celebrate every move-out day together, notify us of job openings and childcare options. They donate food and clothes their kids have grown out of."

She paused as the waitress came to deliver the check, struggling to get her emotions under control. More than anything, she hated to appear weak. As a kid, it had almost gotten her killed. Now, her strength could mean the difference between *Maison de Jardin* remaining a home or becoming a commodity. "I refuse to give up on that."

Even if it meant giving up on her part of it. All her life, she'd only wanted to serve the women in need she saw around her. Just like she and her mother had so desperately needed someone when Michael found them at the hospital. But if having *Maison de Jardin* survive meant she had to move on to the role of director of Hyatt Heights, Inc., then that was what she would do.

Rhett remained quiet as they left the restaurant and slowly walked down the sidewalk. This little café was one of her favorites, tucked away on the side of a hotel in the French Quarter where she could walk around and enjoy the historic buildings, black iron railings and flickering street lamps. Here she could simply think as she strolled. They continued along the street for a while, as she texted Roberto where to meet them. She breathed in the cooler air flowing between the buildings. New Orleans summer heat was rarely kind or forgiving.

"I think what you're doing is incredibly risky," Rhett said. His serious tone disappointed her. Sometimes it was exhausting when people didn't understand you.

She paused, surprised by the rebuke even though she knew many would share his opinion. What she was doing *was* risky. But these women were worth it.

Despite his words, his hands were gentle as he turned her to face him, lifting her chin to get her to look up at him. "If you lose your inheritance, what would happen to *you*? That salary could be all you have to fall back on."

She opened her mouth to defend herself, though she wasn't sure she had the words. He laid a finger over her lips. "But I also think what you're doing is very, very brave."

"I've been without before," she whispered around the tightness in her throat.

"Which just means you know more than others what you're sacrificing." His gray gaze bored into hers, making her want to shift, make any movement that would relieve the tension building inside her. No man had ever looked at her like he did right this moment, with a mixture of admiration and heat that caught her off guard.

She couldn't pull away when he wrapped his palms around her jaw, cupping her face as if it were utterly fragile and utterly precious. Then his mouth covered hers in a firm kiss.

What started out as admiration quickly transformed

into something deeper, something mutual. A restrained version of the night before.

Something Trinity wasn't sure she could resist for long.

Rhett ignored the buzz of his phone in his pocket as he greeted members of Hyatt Heights's board and upper management from the companies the next day. This Saturday crawfish boil at one of the executives' mansions seemed to be the Southern version of putting him on display, replacing the press conference he'd refused to attend.

In true New Orleans fashion, he could hear live jazz playing through the open French doors on the far side of the great hall. The spicy scent of the food being served under the large tents on the back lawn also drifted in, reminding Rhett of his empty stomach. Crawfish boil wasn't his favorite dish, but hopefully he'd get a big bowl of gumbo at some point. He'd become addicted to that and po'boys since he'd come to NOLA.

Hyatt Heights would have hired the best chef in the city. They spared no expense, especially when they were trying to convince their employees that everything was perfectly fine.

Somehow, he had a feeling this crowd was gonna have him too busy shaking hands to truly enjoy the chef's work.

Bill had told him he and Larry wanted a casual environment for him to win over the board members and executives. Any conversations with the upper management would hopefully filter down to employees and set people at ease—or as much at ease as they could be, knowing the ownership of the corporation might be in dispute for a while. They also hoped that these reassurances filtered out to the public from today's event.

After touching base with a couple groups of attendees, Rhett stepped off to the side to check his phone. The entire time he swept his gaze over the room, looking for Trinity. They'd been separated quickly after they'd come in. The longer they were apart, the more Rhett felt anxiety creeping over him.

Then he saw his waiting text message. You were right. Hyatts deep in debt. Details sent via secure email.

Good to know. Chris had done what Rhett asked, even if he had disagreed with what he perceived as Rhett's motive behind it. Frankly, Rhett's train of thought was beginning to worry him a bit, too. For the first time since he'd started in this profession, the very person he'd come to investigate might just be the innocent in the situation.

Though his brain fought the idea, his body seemed to be fully on board, which was troublesome in and of itself.

When he looked up from his phone, he saw the Hyatts bearing down on him. A deep breath helped him brace for what he knew he had to do.

"Let's find a place to talk," Richard said as soon as he was within speaking distance.

"Are you sure?" Rhett asked with a polite smile for anyone who cared to look their way.

Richard didn't need to answer. His wife was busy

answering for him. "Since we're the ones in charge, I don't think it's your place to ask questions."

Rhett simply stared her down. She might think she was in charge, but he had a few tricks up his sleeve she might not be aware of. His quick glance for Trinity came up empty once more.

Richard led them to a nearby office and closed the door after they all filed inside.

"Since you don't seem willing to give us a report otherwise, I think you should do it in person," Patricia said, her tone indicating this was her due.

*Amateurs.* "You and Larry were told you probably wouldn't get an update because of the sensitive and up close nature of this investigation. Doing it this way, in person, actually increases the risk of exposure."

Patricia threw her husband a look. "I don't think we're getting our money's worth."

He wasn't about to let this opportunity pass. "Since you aren't paying my salary, I think you are."

Both looked surprised.

"Didn't think I would realize that, huh?" Rhett was ready to play hardball. "Other than my initial fee, Hyatt Heights is paying my salary as a *business consultant.* Isn't that convenient?"

"You signed a binding contract," Richard insisted.

"That I did," Rhett conceded. "But that contract was separate from the one I signed for consulting. I've waived portions of your fee out of generosity. Would you care to pay your portion?"

Both sputtered at the implications.

"Now, I am continuing my investigations, I assure

you. Because I want Michael's inheritance to go to the rightful person."

"Well, that person is not the woman who married him for his money just a week before he died. Hell, she probably had a hand in killing him."

Rhett didn't bother to comment on that. The investigators of the helicopter crash had easily ruled it an accident. The experienced pilot had flown for Michael for years and lost his own life—it had nothing to do with foul play.

"I will figure out if she married him for his money," he said, "but I do have a few questions for the two of you."

Did he come right out with it? Or take a subtler approach? Patricia and Richard didn't seem the subtle type.

"Why would you question us?" Patricia had the ruffled chicken feathers posture down to an art.

"Because it's important for me to understand what is happening on all sides of the situation." Especially during his unexplained crisis of conscience. "I visited *Maison de Jardin* yesterday. It's a very beautiful, very *valuable* property."

He didn't miss the quick glance the couple exchanged.

Richard was prepared for this subject. "I see you've heard the rumors about how easy it would be to sell the place."

"Of course, it would be," Patricia concurred. "But that's never been our intention."

Rhett wasn't buying it. No one could look at that

place and not wonder what it was worth. "You never encouraged Michael to sell the estate and move the charity to a smaller property?"

"Many times," Patricia said with a wave of her hand. "But that was before. It has nothing to do with us fighting for our rightful place as Michael's heirs."

"Besides, the businesses are worth far more than *Maison de Jardin* would ever be," Richard assured him…a little too glibly.

"But the businesses wouldn't be as easy to liquidate if you needed money."

"That's not an issue," Patricia snapped.

"According to the IRS it is."

She gasped. "We are *not* under investigation here."

That's what she would want him to think. He didn't miss the fact that she didn't dispute what he was saying. "I have to ask *all* the questions. As I've said many times in my career, if you haven't done anything wrong, you have nothing to hide."

"Don't compare us with Trinity and her like," Patricia hissed. "We aren't criminals."

*Yet.*

Richard had a cooler head. "He's right, darlin'. And we have absolutely nothing to hide." He nodded at Rhett. "Yes, our finances have been strained lately, and it's no secret that Michael had many buyers approach him with offers for *Maison de Jardin* through the years. His parents, too." Richard took a few steps closer, meeting Rhett's gaze head-on. "But we simply want what is best for the companies. That's the important part right now."

Patricia's phone dinged while the men stared each other down. Rhett ignored her until she held her phone out to her husband with a smirk. "Well, if you wanted to create even more negative press for her, you're doing pretty well," she said.

Richard's surprised expression didn't bode well. "Yes, sir," he said. "You are certainly good at your job."

Then he turned the screen around so Rhett could see the posted picture of him kissing Trinity.

# Nine

The first giggle didn't quite register. It was just background noise that Trinity easily dismissed.

Then she heard another giggle. Then another, accompanied by a rising swell of murmurings that set her teeth on edge. She was used to this, ever since she'd first gone out in public after Michael's death. But this might be the worst she'd experienced. It was like a dream she'd had as a teenager about walking through the school halls in her pj's with everyone she knew laughing at her when she passed by.

*It might have nothing to do with you.*

But a quick glance around showed furtive looks being thrown her way. It was definitely about her. What horrible thing had that blogger posted now?

Before she could dig her phone out of her pocket-book, Bill appeared at her side. "Trinity, how could you do this?"

*Uh-oh.* "Do what?"

One flash of his phone and heat burned across her cheeks. She didn't even have to see the comments. She could imagine what they were. There she was, in full color, getting hot and heavy with Rhett on a public sidewalk. At least, that's what the picture made it look like. Only the two of them knew the kiss had been brief, and in her mind innocent. While it had been wonderful, it hadn't been an action *inspired* by lust or arousal.

Though it had ultimately sparked both, at least for her.

But she'd felt like it had started as Rhett's way of showing admiration. Something she hadn't had in a long time. No one else knew the context, the conversation that had preceded that small moment in time.

Bill took her arm, leading her back through the house toward the front rooms. They were halfway there when Larry joined them. He shook his phone at them, though the screen was black. "Bill, this is not the impression I was trying to make."

Trinity wished a hole would open up and swallow her. Never having had much of a love life, she wasn't used to it being talked about by anyone, much less by strangers. She'd avoided the spotlight her entire life, only to find herself living in it permanently since Michael's death.

She wasn't sure how much of this she could take. To her dismay, she was finding that her loyalty to him might actually have its limits.

The men continued flanking her on each side, making her feel like she was being escorted out in shame. Her stomach roiled, the smell of spicy food setting off a wave of nausea as her emotions washed over her. How could this be happening? How could Michael have left her to this?

She ducked her head, hoping to hide the tears that welled up. Picking up her pace, she rushed on, just hoping for a bit of privacy before she broke down.

But after a moment, someone stepped into her path. Before she could even look up, she knew it was Rhett. It was his smell. She felt his touch on her arm. She immediately wanted to collapse into his arms and let the world disappear. Which made her straighten her spine and squeeze her eyes shut.

Then she heard Larry from her side. "Isn't our situation enough of a soap opera at the moment? What were you two thinking?"

Would the embarrassments never end?

"Excuse me?" The hard tone of Rhett's voice was a warning Larry ignored.

"The purpose of tonight is to allay our stockholders' fears, soothe our employees' worries." Larry shook his phone. "This doesn't exactly say 'focused on keeping our business stable.'"

"Let's not talk about this in the open," Bill said, leading Trinity into a little alcove near the front door.

She wanted nothing more than to just bolt out the door and be done with today.

Larry trailed behind them. "You've embarrassed us, Trinity," he scolded.

Rhett pivoted to face him. "Do not talk to her like that. It's uncalled for."

They all stood frozen for a moment. Trinity could barely breathe for the emotions squeezing her chest. Until now, only two people had ever stood up for her during her lifetime. One was her mother. She'd done it quietly, with actions rather than her words. Michael had done it through support, but never direct confrontation.

But here was Rhett defending her out in the open.

"Look," he went on, "the kiss was a simple thank-you. Not the seduction that picture makes it look like."

He glanced back toward the crowds in the open space of the living area. Here and there, someone looked their way but no one had made a move to pursue them. "Even if it had been, we're adults. What happened yesterday should have been between the two of us. Not between us and the whole world."

"Not when her husband just died and we are fighting for his inheritance," Larry hissed.

The two men stared each other down as they jockeyed for dominance.

Bill's voice was much softer. "It does look bad."

"Public opinion doesn't sway a judge," Rhett insisted.

The slow shake of Bill's head made Trinity's stomach sink. "This is the South. It depends on the judge."

Rhett squeezed the bridge of his nose between his thumb and forefinger, blowing out a deep breath. "Right now," he finally said, "we just need to get Trinity out of here."

Larry straightened with an almost audible snap. "That defeats the purpose of this little shindig."

Trinity let her gaze find Rhett's. She could feel her mask falling into place. The same one she'd used to tell her daddy she didn't care how much he yelled and hit her. The same one she donned in the boardroom when Richard and Patricia flung insults at her. The mask that hid the real feelings that people only used against her.

"It's okay," she said. Even though she knew it would be hours before she could seek the safety and solitude of her suite at Hyatt House.

Rhett searched her face with his gray-green eyes, making her wonder if he could see beyond the mask to the humiliation and pain beneath. She hoped not.

He nodded enigmatically. Then he stepped across their little circle to wrap his arm around her shoulders. "If that's the case, we will go all in," he announced.

He led her away from the little group, but he didn't let go as they paused at the top of the steps leading into the living area. If anything, he pulled her a little closer.

She glanced up at him, unsure what he was planning. His proximity sent shivers down her spine despite the twenty pairs of eyes turned in their direction. "What should I do?" she asked, desperate for even an ounce of the calm demeanor he seemed to have adopted like a well-worn sweater.

He smiled down at her, a look so intimate it took her breath away. The feel of his arm holding her close was the most secure she'd felt in her entire life.

"Hold your head high, Trinity." Then he led her into the crowd.

* * *

A week later, Rhett strode down the hall of Hyatt House, irritation feeding his quick stride. This was the third morning in a row that Trinity had missed breakfast and he was having no more of it. She was coming to breakfast if he had to carry her there.

He knew where she would be. The library or the office. He'd found her in both places for the last few days, crouched over books he'd recommended or drawing up notes and plans for the businesses. While he admired her dedication—he'd rarely seen a CEO more dedicated than she was—he had to admit he was worried.

First, she was avoiding him. After all the attention from the *NOLA Secrets & Scandals* blog post, he *shouldn't* blame her. But he did. Her avoidance left him aching to see her, talk to her and, if he was honest, touch her again.

Second, she was working herself into an illness.

He walked through Michael's empty office into Trinity's. There she was, behind her desk. Only she wasn't really sitting. Instead she was propping herself up by her arms and shoulders on the cluttered desktop. Her face was buried in a book, but she wasn't reading. Her hair fanned over her face, hiding her closed eyes from view.

Rhett paused for a moment, almost in awe of the softening he felt in his chest. No matter how much his brain said it was dangerous, he couldn't fight it. He admired her determination, her loyalty and her grace under pressure. The way she pushed herself to learn and grow for the good of people she would probably never meet.

It was so unlike how he'd first heard her described:

as a charity director who had conned a billionaire into marrying her.

He slowly advanced across the room, uncertainty slowing his steps. What should he do? Part of him wanted to carry her to bed. His intentions weren't entirely pure, but he had a feeling the only way she'd stay there would be if he wrapped her up in his arms and held her still until sleep became irresistible. He could just imagine her soft warmth molding against him as she surrendered to the rest her body needed so badly.

But then all his pure intentions would probably go up in smoke.

Should he wake her? Find a way to make her more comfortable where she was? She'd wake up with a terrible backache once her nap was over. It was hardly restful.

For the first time in his career—hell, since the moment he'd realized his fiancée was preparing to take him for all he was worth—he put aside his suspicions and let himself feel.

He felt the weight of responsibility and a touch of guilt that he had given her what was essentially busy work to satisfy a bunch of men who couldn't believe in her. He felt admiration for her hard work and dedication. He felt an anxious need to touch her in a way she'd never forget.

What was that about? It was certainly something he'd never felt before. Something he dared not put into words...even in his own mind. But that didn't mean he wouldn't act on it.

Steeling himself against what could only be a weakness, he strode across the quiet space. With a firm touch, he rubbed her back until she stirred in the chair. It took a few moments before her eyes opened. Even then, she looked up with a hazy cloud over her gaze that warned him she wasn't fully awake.

Was she always like this? Would he need to kiss her awake in the mornings, slowly bringing her to consciousness in a sweetly sensual way? Or was she normally an eager riser, with this haziness only brought on by too many late nights and too much studying?

He knelt beside her chair. "Good morning, Sleeping Beauty. It's time for breakfast."

She looked cute with her unguarded frown and wayward hair cascading in all directions.

What the hell was he thinking?

He firmed his tone. "You will come eat. We'll discuss what needs to happen next after you have some food in you."

She stood, self-consciously tugging at her rumpled clothes and smoothing down her hair. Her balance still seemed a little unsteady as they made their way back down the hall.

"How late were you up last night?" he asked, his tone hushed to match the quiet atmosphere of the house before the bustle of the day.

She mumbled a little, probably expecting to get away with not really answering, but he paused and looked down at her. He wouldn't have asked the question if he didn't want the answer.

Her gaze skittered away from his before settling

somewhere on the floor ahead of them. "Three…maybe four. I'm not sure."

Yes, this definitely had to stop.

When they got to the dining room, she simply dropped into the chair at the table and stared out the window onto the rain-soaked patio. Only one of the French doors was open this morning, letting in the sweet, cool breeze. He filled her plate with eggs, fruit and the biscuit with strawberry jam and butter she had every morning. To his relief, she dug right in without complaint. He waited until she had a good portion in her before he started.

"You're taking on too much," he said, not bothering to beat around the bush.

Her confused look wrinkled her adorable brow. "I have to prove I'm competent."

And he'd been a party to making her feel that way, something he could now admit he regretted. "At the expense of your health? Your ability to think and reason? All of that diminishes with lack of sleep, exercise and food. Then where will you be? Where will the residents of *Maison de Jardin* be?"

He let a touch of irritation creep into his voice. "On top of that, you've been giving up your salary. I'm all for helping others, but your sense of self-preservation seems to have gone right out the window. You're too sensible for that."

For the first time, Rhett got to see anger flush those gorgeous cheeks. She narrowed her eyes but couldn't hide her tears. "I don't understand what you want from me," she said through clenched teeth.

"For you to cut yourself a break."

Her irritation was replaced by a look of surprise. He had to wonder if anyone had ever bothered taking care of her, instead of her always being the responsible one. Had Michael ever pampered her? Loved on her?

"Look, you're working very hard. But if you burn out, you can't help anyone, can you?"

Her shoulders slumped, which made him feel like a bully. But this was important, dammit!

"You need rest and a day off."

She looked skeptical.

"An entire day," he insisted.

"I don't know."

How could he tempt her? "If you could do anything fun, what would it be?"

She didn't even hesitate. "I'd go to the movies."

He hadn't expected that. He'd rarely seen her watch television—she was always so focused on books and paperwork. "I'm not sure if being in public is a good idea, but we'll make it work." Maybe he could rent out a theater for the day?

A small grin, her first for the day, tugged at her bow-shaped lips. "Actually, follow me. I have a surprise for you."

# Ten

Trinity headed into the theater room, energy in her step for the first time since Rhett had woken her up at her desk. She heard his quick intake of breath and smiled. It was the same reaction she had to this room every time she walked through the door.

"Michael had this built for me," she said, her voice hushed as if not to disturb the memories that lingered here.

She'd spent so many nights here beside her best friend, watching the latest action releases, laughing over old comedies and peeking through her fingers at the villain on the big screen. But in truth, she didn't want the reminder of her dead husband to cast shadows on this moment.

Michael had gone all in on an old-fashioned theater

look: velvet curtains, iron lantern fixtures, and a full-wall screen. But the seating was modern. In the center of the room was a comfortable-looking oversize power lounger big enough for two. Pairs of oversize leather recliners were lined up around it from the screen to the back wall. Trinity strolled over to it and pushed a single button. With a whir of machinery, the top half dropped all the way back so the viewer could actually lie down if she wanted.

"This is incredible," Rhett said.

Trinity couldn't help but smile. "Michael had two rooms combined to make this theater about five years ago. He claimed it was perfect for entertaining, but we both knew he did this for me. I love watching movies. It's my favorite way to unwind. But he didn't like going to an actual theater because of crowds and travel time and such, so this was the compromise."

Rhett cocked his head to the side to study her. "I never would have pegged you for a movie buff."

"All it took was one good movie and I was hooked," she said, smiling at the memory. "As I mentioned before, my mother was very religious. Extremely conservative. She believed that movies were sinful. So was television unless it was the news. I wasn't allowed to watch anything. Not even cartoons."

"That must have been weird when all of your friends were talking about the latest TV show."

She shrugged. "Honestly, I spent a lot of time reading, so it didn't bother me much until I became a teenager. The whole 'being different' thing made me even more of an outsider than our low income did." She couldn't suppress a sheepish grin. "But once I got older, I would sneak away to the dollar theater and spend the day watching movie after movie. It was wonderfully decadent."

Rhett moved closer, close enough she imagined she felt the heat radiating off his body. Part of her had a hard time believing they were having this conversation. Was he really interested? Or just humoring her?

"Anyway, now I don't have to leave the house to watch movies." Trinity gestured around the room. "I can indulge whenever I want."

"When was the last time you did?"

Everything inside her went still. She forced the words out through her tight throat. "Michael and I had movie night a couple of days before he died."

Without noticing him move, Trinity realized Rhett was almost touching her. "This looks like the perfect place to spend a rainy day," he said, his voice soothing, coaxing her to relax.

"I have so much I need to do today," she objected, feeling the familiar guilt over taking a day off.

"And it will still be there tomorrow."

"My mother always said that was a lazy person's excuse." And she'd been fond of saying so.

"That explains this strange complex you have." Rhett placed his hand on her back. The concentrated heat she remembered upon waking this morning returned, loosening her muscles, pulling her into the plan. "But I think this is the perfect place to spend a day relaxing, renewing your energy. Don't you?"

She looked around the shadowy room, imagining

the joy of spending an entire day indulging her favorite pastime. "With buttery popcorn?"

"I think Frederick might be able to scare us up some. Maybe lunch, too."

"Us? Will you join me?" She swallowed, afraid to look at Rhett. If she saw rejection in those gray eyes in her fragile state, it just might cause a breakdown.

He was silent for so long, her fear multiplied. She had to force herself to meet his gaze, braced for what she might see. Even in the shadows, she could make out the crinkle of laugh lines around his eyes as he smiled.

"I wouldn't miss it," he said.

Why was her heart speeding as if she'd run a race?

"Now," he went on, "go upstairs, change into some lounging clothes and bring whatever you need to be comfortable for the day back here. I'll look over the movie selection."

"If you're joining me, you need to change, too." She dared to let her gaze stray over the button-down shirt and dress pants he sported.

His grin only grew bigger. "You're on."

Trinity took a few extra minutes for a quick shower to wash off the last of the grunge from sleeping in her clothes. Then she put on her softest lounge pants and T-shirt and returned to the theater room carrying her pillow and blanket. She tried not to think about a day spent watching movies with a man who made her heart race and her palms perspire. If he enjoyed this as much as she did, she might be completely hooked.

More than anything, she forcefully pushed away the guilt of letting her work slide for the day. As Rhett had said, it would still be there tomorrow. And nothing urgent was pending at the moment, so this wouldn't do any harm.

The thought of taking a mental break made her want to whimper in relief. Her head felt overstuffed from studying, and she was exhausted from trying to create profitable, secure scenarios for Hyatt Heights's future. She needed rest. She knew that… She'd just been afraid to take the time off.

Trinity dumped her pillow-blanket combo, then moved over to where Rhett was perusing the list of movie choices. She felt a little more comfortable at the sight of the lounge pants and plain white T-shirt he'd put on. She peered past his arm to see what part of the list he'd made it to, recognizing it right away.

"What about a superhero marathon?"

He glanced back at her in surprise. "Are you just saying that because I'm a guy?"

"Why would you think that?"

"It's just not the kind of movies I would have expected you to like."

"Why?" She slapped her hands on her hips in mock indignation. "Because I'm a girl?"

"*Touché.*"

"What kind of movies do you think I actually like?" She was almost afraid to find out.

"You know, romances or tearjerkers."

"So cliché." Trinity shrugged. "I got into superheroes at *Maison de Jardin*. We as residents didn't need a ton of extra emotion, and romances were excluded on sheer principle, since most of the women there were in the first throws of broken relationships. What we needed most were calls to action. There's nothing more inspiring in that department than superhero movies."

"You're a girl after my own heart."

She wondered if she really could be.

"Uh-uh. Phone off."

The side-eye she cast him was just adorable.

"I'm serious," Rhett said. "The last thing you need is a text message making more demands on you or a phone call with bad news. We've had enough nasty surprises over the last couple of weeks."

And that was an understatement. But he'd pushed her enough for today. He simply watched in silence while she contemplated the empty screen of her phone. Hopefully the promise of a drama-free day would convince her to just turn it off.

Sure enough, she eased her thumb to the off button and held it down.

"Good girl."

She gave him a piercing glance. "Now you," she demanded.

Turnabout was fair play.

Rhett didn't usually turn off his phone for anyone. Yes, he might have a slight addiction, but he needed his gadgets to stay on top of his game. But under Trinity's mock-stern gaze, he, too, shut down his link to the outside world.

As he watched her create a little nest on her side of the lounger by raising the headrest to a decent angle and draping a soft fluffy blanket over the cushion, he wondered what came next. Would he be expected to keep his hands to himself with this sexy woman right beside him? *Boring.* But how was he supposed to know how far to take this?

Excitement and a touch of unease tightened his gut.

His uncertainty almost got the better of him as he stood beside the lounger not moving even after she settled in and pushed the button to start the first movie. But when she glanced up at him, it broke through his inertia. He sat down beside her. Close but not touching. Not nearly close enough.

They were about thirty minutes in before she passed the tub of buttery popcorn to him and asked, "So what do you think?"

"Definitely the most unique date I've had." His entire body tightened as he realized what he'd just said.

He was almost afraid to look over and see her reaction. She'd gone so still, he thought at first she might be angry. A quick glance proved she was watching him instead of the screen, but her expression was guarded in the flickering lights.

"Is it a date?" she finally asked.

He wished he had a prepared statement ready. "Would that be a problem?"

She reached for another handful of popcorn and chewed thoughtfully before answering. He couldn't tell if it was a delay tactic. "We *are* working together."

Two could stall. He munched on his popcorn for a minute or two, enjoying the salty, buttery goodness.

Finally he said, "On the other hand, we've already spread the idea that we're an item around to most of the

people who know you. Even some people who don't."
He indulged in another handful of popcorn as he reflected on the crawfish boil Saturday, when he'd put
his arm around her and they went out to face the hostile, curious crowd together. Signaling that there was
something going on between them.

Was he meant to be a white knight instead of a
sneaky spy?

"I say we go with it." This time he wasn't playing
around. Something deep inside was driving this. It was
time he owned up to it. "I want to see where this leads."

"I thought you were just being nice at the party, getting me out of an awkward jam."

He'd thought so, too, at first. He took a deep breath
as he waded into deeper waters. "I wasn't sure at the
time why I did that. Normally I would never take that
step, especially publicly. I drew a hard line in the sand
a long time ago. I don't sleep with clients… I certainly
don't get involved."

"Because of your fiancée?"

Rhett's gut contracted as if she'd hit him square in
the stomach. He'd left himself unguarded, and she got
in.

"I'm sorry," she quickly followed up. "I didn't mean
to pry—"

"No." In for a penny… "You've had your private life
made very public. I'm just not used to talking about
mine."

"Was she involved in your business?"

"Not that I was aware of." He hadn't meant that to
sound quite so bitter. In all honesty, he wasn't harbor-

ing a lot of resentment. He had in the beginning, but he'd channeled all of that negative energy into building his current business.

"I don't understand," Trinity said, distracting him from his thoughts.

He cleared his throat, trying to formulate the most straightforward answer. "I found out that what she really wanted me for was my bank account. I was her chance to live the high life without having to do any of the work." He stared at the flickering screen without really seeing it. "It's a lousy feeling—one I wouldn't wish on anyone."

"No one wants to be used," Trinity said, her voice almost lost in a loud explosion from the movie. "Or accused of being a user. That's what I don't understand—do Richard and Patricia really think Michael wasn't smart enough to defend himself against something like that?"

"I wasn't."

She was silent for a moment before she asked, "Did you know her long?"

He shook his head. "Less than a year."

"Michael and I had been friends for over fifteen."

Rhett needed to start trusting that Michael had known what he was doing.

Her gentle tone contrasted sharply with the loud sounds from the screen as she went on, "I'm sorry you went through that. Once that faith in others is broken—I know from experience that getting it back is hard. Especially with no one to lean on."

Rhett liked to think he didn't need anyone for that, but didn't everyone? "Men are a little different than women in that regard, I think," he said, ignoring the gruffness that crept into his voice.

"I'm sure they like to think so."

He glanced over at her but her smile was soft, encouraging rather than judgmental. "How would you know?" he teased. "Didn't you grow up in a house full of women?"

"Human nature is what it is."

He'd always thought so. Now he wasn't so sure.

# Eleven

She was so warm.

It had been years since Trinity had felt this kind of snuggly, secure warmth that made her want to burrow in and hide from the light of day. Or rather, the light from the movie screen.

Consciousness slowly returned as she became aware of the source of both the light and sound. The flashes against her closed eyelids made her want to turn away from the intrusion, toward the source of the heat at her side. Toward the smell of citrus and musk.

She forced her eyelids up.

Under other circumstances, opening her eyes to the sight of a man lying beside her would have been shocking. It was disconcerting…since it had never happened to her before. But something about knowing this man was Rhett Brannon settled her mind then and there. This might be new. Just a little bit scary... Okay, a lot. But she didn't want to be anywhere else but beside him.

He wasn't pushing her away, so maybe he felt the same.

She could tell from the soundtrack that they'd reached about the middle of the third movie. She wasn't sure when she'd fallen asleep, but obviously she'd taken liberties and made Rhett serve as a pillow. Did he mind?

A squeal of tires on the big screen sent a shock through her. Involuntarily her fingers curled into his chest as if to give herself an anchor. She watched in fascination as his hand drifted up to cover hers.

If possible, she relaxed even more.

"Sleep well?"

The vibration of his chest beneath her palm as he spoke prompted her to rub small circles in his cotton T-shirt. She swallowed down her shyness and tilted her head back until she could see his face. "Yes," she admitted. "Um, thanks for providing a replacement pillow?"

He grinned, his teeth flashing white in the dim shadows. "No problem. I stole yours anyway."

He reached out and pushed her hair back away from her face. It must have come loose while she slept. Her heart sped up as his fingers tugged on the silky strands, then even more as he rolled to his side, easing her back against the cushions.

The headrest of the lounger was still elevated so they were level with each other but she still felt dwarfed by him. Not physically, but because of his intensity.

His hooded gaze stole her breath. She couldn't look away.

"Trinity?" he said, his voice a soft question that surprised her.

He was asking for permission to continue and she found herself considering whether she should give it. Some women might not bother thinking about it. She imagined them throwing themselves at this willing man lying next to her with abandon. But Trinity had never been that carefree.

Rhett had proven he cared about her. It wasn't about a quick roll in the hay. He'd supported her through some difficult situations. Today alone said that he cared about her as a person, rather than just a convenient body. Was that enough?

Instead of passively offering her permission, Trinity reached up to rub her thumb along the strong edge of his jaw. Rough stubble scratched her fingertips. What would that scruff feel like against more tender skin? Against her belly or her thighs?

His eyes slowly closed, but otherwise he didn't move as her hand wandered down to the side of his neck. She indulged her curiosity, running her fingers through his hair, testing the textures. The dark hair against the nape of his neck was softer; the gray coming in at his temples tended more toward coarseness. She trailed her touch to his full lips, then down over his chin.

She let her palm fall to his shirt once more, detecting the faint texture of chest hair through the fabric. As she approached his belly button, his stomach tightened, the muscles rippling beneath her touch. She wanted so badly to close her eyes and focus on the feel of him, but she couldn't drag her gaze away from the expression on his face.

It wasn't pain or ecstasy but almost a surprised fascination. She didn't know how else to describe it. He practically soaked in her touch.

She shifted so she could use both hands. She pressed her palms into his muscles, testing the resistance. The feel of him leaning into her touch sent a thrill through her. She followed the corded muscle of his chest out to his shoulders and grasped them with an intensity that conveyed exactly what she wanted from him.

He followed her lead, leaning forward to kiss her forehead. Then he brushed his lips over her brows, her cheekbones, exploring her just as she had explored him.

Finally, his lips brushed hers, the tang of salt giving way to sweet surrender. She pulled him closer, her grip tightening. The ache of need spread through her body.

He didn't hurry. He took his time exploring her mouth. The dance of lips and tongue set off tingles that spread in waves over her skin.

She couldn't hold back the moan from deep in her throat. Everything he did felt so good. Better than she'd ever imagined.

He moved even lower, letting his body slide against hers, producing delicious friction. She felt the heat of his mouth against her throat. Her hips rose against him without her permission. So intoxicating.

Mewling sounds escaped her as he licked along her neck, then suckled gently right below her ear. She gasped, clutching him to her. She wanted, no, needed, him closer. She tilted her head back, giving him an all-access pass.

Only then did she realize that a light was intruding on the darkness. Opening her eyes, she realized the movie was over and the wall sconces had automatically turned on. They weren't super bright, but it felt like it.

She tried closing her eyes again. Tried focusing in on Rhett—the feel of him, the heat of him. Instead her mind started to race. What if someone came in? What if she did something stupid? What if something went wrong?

And was she ready to expose her most intimate secret to him? The thought rolled over and over in her brain, leaving her whimpering.

This had to stop. She had to stop. Panic sped up her heartbeat, left her gasping.

Some of it must have gotten through to Rhett because he pulled back just enough to look down at her. "Everything okay?" he asked.

She wanted it to be… More than anything. But her brain simply wouldn't shut off. She licked her lips. What should she do?

"Trinity?" he said, once again stroking her hair back from her face.

She didn't want to say it out loud, but her body chose for her. "No, I'm not okay."

Even as she tried to rein in her panic, Trinity felt it slipping through her grasp. Control was a thing of beauty in her world. The one thing that allowed her to steer in the face of wave after wave that threatened to capsize her boat. Right now, as her heart raced out of control and she struggled to breathe, control seemed forever out of her grasp.

She pulled away, pressing her palms into the soft cushions as she forced breath in and out of her lungs. She tried stretching to relieve the tightness from her back and neck, anchoring herself to keep from losing her balance. But it wasn't the physical symptoms that were the most daunting—it was the constant racing of her thoughts.

Why wouldn't they stop?

"Trinity," Rhett said from the opposite side of the lounger. His voice wavered as her brain cried out for more oxygen, making it a struggle to understand his words. "What's the matter?"

But she couldn't tell him. Nothing would allow her to voice the fears his touch evoked. It was a can of worms she simply wasn't ready to open. After all, she'd spent the last eight weeks pretending to be the epitome of Michael's true love. She knew she'd been his closest friend. She'd told others time and again that she'd been his best friend. But that wasn't what they wanted to hear. She was either his one true love…or a gold digger.

To tell anyone that she was still a virgin after becoming a widow would shatter the illusion of why she and Michael had married…because no one wanted to hear the truth.

Knowing that she wouldn't be able to hide that knowledge from Rhett if she slept with him wasn't something she was ready to deal with. The last thing she wanted was to rehash her relationship with her husband right after having sex with someone else.

She clenched her fists into the cool silkiness of the cushions, forcing herself to focus on the tangible connection as she continued drawing air in and out. In and out. In and out.

"I'm sorry," she finally gasped. Which felt juvenile and lame. What woman has a panic attack because a sexy man wants to touch her?

What was wrong with her?

"I'm sorry," she said again, her voice steadier this time. "I just started thinking…and I couldn't stop."

He stood nearby, dwarfing her with his height. "That doesn't sound like the result I was looking for."

The amused tone in his voice at least cut the tension a notch. "Yeah," she gasped. "Not helpful."

"Do you need anything?"

"This is gonna sound nuts." And probably was, but she couldn't talk about her biggest concern. Not openly. So she moved on to the next one. "But I started to think about some person, some photographer, suddenly jumping out of the shadows and taking pictures of me. Of us. Isn't that crazy?"

"I hope that doesn't happen. That's the last thing I want people to watch me doing." He laughed.

"Hey, what about me?" she asked with fake indignation. It was easier than focusing on her panic attack, and she was grateful to him for leading them in a less intense direction.

He shrugged. "I'm pretty sure you'll be beautiful regardless of what you're doing."

"Flatterer."

As self-conscious as that made her feel, at least they weren't dwelling on her other issues...

But Rhett wasn't about to be kept at arm's length for long. He reached out and wrapped his arms around her shoulders. His warmth at her side made her feel supported, but it wasn't sexual in any way. She hooked her hands over his forearm draped across her front, anchoring herself.

"You probably think I'm being overly dramatic," she finally said.

He rested his forehead briefly against hers before straightening again. "Look, everything has happened very quickly," he acknowledged. "I understand that. You've barely had time to mourn your husband."

Trinity felt a jolt burst through her. Her husband. Difficult to remember. Hard to forget.

"And now all of this other stuff with the businesses and charity and the press." He squeezed her against him for a moment. "I think being touchy and emotional is a normal response."

"That's making allowances," she said, hearing echoes of her mother's stern voice in her words.

Rhett shook his head in denial. "No. Most days you're regal, moving through it all with a poise I can only envy. But everyone is human. Even you."

She lifted her chin so she could stare at him.

"What?" he asked.

"Michael used to say that," she answered, reluctant to bring him up but needing to be honest. *Just try your best. Everybody makes mistakes.* "He didn't accept deliberate slacking, but he also remembered that the people around him had limits."

"Sounds like a smart man."

At first, she thought Rhett was retreating as his grip loosened but then he eased one of his large hands around her to rub her back. He gave her comfort. Something she'd had very little of in her life…and none since she'd lost Michael. Would Rhett understand what that meant for her?

"He was my best friend," she said, hating that she sounded lost, forlorn. She couldn't help but wonder what Rhett would say if he found out that Michael hadn't been more than that.

Rhett's touch at the base of her neck distracted her from her worries. "Don't worry about this, Trinity," he said.

She barely suppressed a huff of laughter. Rhett added his own chuckle.

"I know. Easier said than done." He tipped her chin up to look into her eyes. "But there's no obligation here. No plan going forward. Take your time to think it through, and decide what you really want. Okay?"

Trinity nodded, but deep inside, she feared this was a choice she wasn't ready to make.

# Twelve

Trinity smiled as Roberto helped Madison into the back of the limo the following evening. The redhead looked flushed but beautiful in her silky lavender gown. Not a look Madison was used to sporting. At *Maison de Jardin*, they normally favored yoga pants or jeans, but this was something the younger woman needed to get used to if she was going to represent the charity at fund-raising events.

"Ready?" Rhett asked with a smile. He was sitting next to Trinity on the plush leather back seat.

Madison raised a skeptical brow. "No."

Trinity couldn't hold back a small chuckle. She knew the other woman well.

Madison smiled a little. "I'm not a huge fan of crowds," she conceded. "Spending most of your life in a sickroom will do that." She rushed on, as if she wanted to change the subject. "But I'm really grateful that you offered me an invite. And this dress!" She fingered the material, testing the smooth texture. "It's so gorgeous, Trinity. Thank you."

Trinity smiled over the nervous chatter, remembering her own first society fund-raiser. She'd been a bit younger than Madison, and definitely more soft-spoken, but she understood the nerves that came with the job. Having Michael at her side had only helped a little. "It's okay. Just relax. And remember, I'll be right there with you." She glanced over at Rhett. "Have I mentioned this is Madison's first event?"

"I never would have guessed it." He winked at the younger woman. "You look gorgeous, Madison."

Definitely a flatterer.

"Don't worry," he went on. "You'll soon realize it's always just the same boring people talking about the same boring things—"

Trinity cut him off. "You're making it worse. She's starting to turn green."

They all laughed, which helped Madison's color return to normal. The lush foliage, wrought iron gates and decorative stone and brick of the Garden District floated by as Roberto drove them at a leisurely pace to their destination.

"So you live in the Garden District but don't go to the upper-crust parties?" Rhett teased, making Trinity want to elbow him in the side. She knew he was trying to provide a distraction, but worried Madison wouldn't want to discuss her history with a stranger.

"My family used to be pretty well-known," Madison conceded with only a slight hesitation. "But after my mom died, my father withdrew from almost all social contact. Then he got sick, so…"

"I'm sorry to hear that," Rhett said.

She shrugged and said, "It doesn't bother me. I'd rather be useful than pretty, as my father used to say." She paused to nibble on her lip for a moment. "What if I don't know what to say? I mean, it's not like these people will be interested in how I can feed twenty people every day or coordinate their laundry."

The women shared a smile as Trinity remembered her own challenges juggling the two sides of the job. The practicalities of running a charity for women and children were worlds away from anything the glamorous people who supported it had to deal with.

"A lot of it is listening," Rhett offered. "Everyone wants to be heard, right? Listen and pay attention. Offer your unique perspective on whatever the subject matter is."

Trinity knew that advice to be sound. "If I've learned anything in the last few months, it's that you don't need to be formally educated to have an opinion. A lot of people at these events have advanced degrees but no practical experience. Just bring that to the table and know you have an insider's view of what charities like ours need on a day-to-day basis."

Surprising Trinity with a quick kiss, Rhett winked at Madison. "But it helps to have someone beautiful and intelligent at your side."

Trinity glanced down, her heart picking up speed at

the sight of Rhett's hand clasped around her own. He'd decided to fully embrace whatever this was between them and didn't seem worried about providing more fodder for the press.

She'd prefer not to appear on a certain blogger's website again, but wondered what else could possibly be done to her at this point. She'd been called a gold digger, a hooker, a woman willing to use her body to get what she wanted from a young age. Couldn't get much worse than that.

She hoped, since this was a ticketed, private event at a private home, she didn't have any worries on that front tonight.

As if he could read her mind, Rhett squeezed her hand, drawing her attention up to his gaze. He lowered his voice so only she could hear. "Worried?"

"Should I be?" Why she wanted to appear brave to him, she wasn't sure. He'd seen the worst of her fears, anxieties and exhaustion. Who was she kidding?

"No." His gray gaze was steady on her. "I say go all in. Give 'em what they want to see."

She worried at her lower lip, probably ruining her carefully applied lipstick. His attempts to take care of her went straight to her heart. "It's easier to fade into the background."

"They aren't going to let you, are they?"

She shook her head, acknowledging the truth. Richard and Patricia wouldn't stop with their accusations. They'd take every piece of evidence they could find and twist it to support their own version of events. They wanted to make her out to be a grasping harpy who stole their inheritance from them, and threatened the livelihood of thousands of families, when in truth they would simply drain Hyatt Heights of every last ounce of profit they could, all while pretending to be innocent.

It would support their version of the story if she were seen as moving on from her husband in an unseemly amount of time. Never truly mourning him, though she'd mourned him for months before he'd actually died. That was their twisted truth.

But she looked at Rhett and knew of the truth. Someone so supportive and understanding couldn't be a threat to her. She could trust him to help her find her way, and a way for the company, without being swayed by media coverage. As she glanced back down at their intertwined hands, she realized that's what she wanted. It was exactly what she needed in this moment.

But was she brave enough to take what he was offering?

Rhett should have had a moment of downtime while Madison and Trinity made a trip to the ladies' room, but one gesture from Richard over near a back hallway changed all that.

Rhett's thoughts churned as he crossed the crowded room. More than anything, he knew he couldn't give the Hyatts what they wanted. Trinity just wasn't that kind of woman—the sneaky, conniving woman they wanted her to be. And he couldn't portray her that way for any amount of money.

The boisterous music from the live band clashed with Rhett's inner worries.

The fact that he was taking a target's side like this for the first time in his career still left him a little off-kilter. But this wasn't just about his attraction to her. Even if he wasn't with Trinity in the long run, he would stand by her side to the end of her ordeal.

He just hadn't figured out how he would do that yet.

After all, he had signed a contract with the Hyatts. His salary wasn't paid by them, now that he was being paid as a consultant for Hyatt Heights, but he could only imagine what it would do to Trinity to realize he'd been hired to spy on her, not "consult" with her on Hyatt Heights's businesses. And that was a conundrum he hadn't figured out how to fix…yet.

Rhett followed the Hyatts and Larry into a small anteroom that blocked some of the noise from the main hall. No sooner had the trio surrounded him than Richard pounced. "We want more information. Why haven't you found anything yet?"

*Because there's nothing to find.* "I don't have anything of interest to report."

Patricia took two steps and was in his face, anger pinching her already narrow features. "Then you aren't trying hard enough. Everything can be twisted to tell a story, if you just look at it from the right angle."

Larry cleared his throat. "Now, wait a minute…"

"We're running out of time," Patricia said over him, not bothering to keep her voice lowered. "I want evidence now, not when you're done having your way with her."

Rhett's control slipped a notch, pushing him to straighten up and brace himself. "Do *not* speak about her that way."

"We can still use it to our advantage," Patricia said, her expression turning sly. She reached out and gripped one of his biceps with her red-tipped fingers. "Just give 'em some more pictures. A new boyfriend eight weeks after the tragic death of her husband always looks bad." She shared a glance with her husband. "That should shine a light on her true motives, right?"

"What?" Larry exclaimed.

"Shut up." Patricia was determined to run the show. Her nails dug a little deeper. "We want evidence. I don't care what kind it is."

Larry's expression grew panicked. "I do."

Richard carefully pried his wife's talons away from Rhett's arm. "I think we can all work together here. Especially considering the new member of our team."

Rhett narrowed his gaze on the man's face. "What are you talking about?"

"We put out some feelers on that gossip blogger…" Rhett's glare didn't seem to faze Richard. In fact, the man seemed to relish the tension growing in the small room. "And made arrangements for him to be here tonight."

"So it's a man?" Rhett asked.

Patricia wasn't fussy about details. "Don't know. Don't care. As long as you give him or her some good photos tonight, it will keep the controversy going."

"Since you enjoyed the last kiss so much, surely you

wouldn't mind providing another," Richard said with a smirk.

While kissing Trinity was never a hardship, the last thing he wanted was to put her on display. "I don't think—"

"You don't need to think," Patricia interrupted. "Simply do as you're told."

Rhett straightened, unable to stop himself from looming over the thin woman. "You don't seem to understand my job here. I'm an investigator, not some flunky here to *make up* evidence for you."

This time Patricia let her pointed red nail creep down his chest, forcing Rhett to subdue a shudder. "I'm sure Trinity would be interested to learn this about you. Don't you think?"

Richard chimed in, "Or we can find someone more accommodating to do it for us."

Rhett wasn't ready for that. He needed more time to figure out how to get them out of this mess with the least amount of damage to Trinity.

"So you want what? Me to pose for a photo with her so they can shame her again?"

Larry edged toward the wall, a frown marring his normal good ol' boy expression.

Patricia smiled, seeming to sense imminent victory. "Just prove what the world—and the board—already suspect. She's just in it for the money and doesn't care what happens to Hyatt Heights or the family name. You're at least good for that much…or should we find something else on Trinity for the blogger to expose?"

The look the couple shared said they already had

something devious in mind. Rhett worried he couldn't keep the disgust from his expression much longer. Better to keep his mouth shut, for now.

"Just think about it. I'm sure you'll make the right decision," Patricia said before she sipped her pink martini and walked away.

Richard gave him a stern look before following her out into the bustling party.

Larry patted at his sweaty forehead with a handkerchief, looking on the verge of tears. "I didn't mean for this to happen."

"What? Finding yourself in league with the villains?"

"I didn't mean for Trinity to get hurt. I just wanted to scare her into doing the right thing."

Rhett wanted to explode, but forced himself to keep calm. How could Michael have left Trinity surrounded by these people? "How is scaring her the right thing? Or turning the companies over to those people? Is that what you think is right for Michael's legacy?"

Larry pressed the handkerchief over his mouth, letting his head drop forward. Emotions turned his cheeks ruddy. "What should I do?"

It seemed obvious to Rhett but he spelled it out anyway. "Get started swaying the board in her favor…and find me that blogger."

Rhett returned to the party to find Trinity standing next to a high-top table by the dance floor. He followed her gaze to see Madison watching the dancers, a tall man at her side. "Do we know him?" he asked as he placed his hand at the small of Trinity's back.

"Actually, no," she said, studying the couple. "I haven't seen him on the charity circuit before." She turned to Rhett and was silent for a moment. Her smile slowly faded. "Are you okay?"

"Yes." Rhett struggled to clear his throat. The last thing he wanted was to put Trinity on display, but he didn't trust Patricia not to do something harmful if he didn't comply. He wished he didn't have to do this. "You look beautiful," he said, regret tightening his throat once more.

"Thank you. You aren't too bad to look at yourself."

"Then let's not waste this moment. How about a dance?" That should provide plenty of interesting pictures.

Trinity eyed the antics on the dance floor with a skeptical look. "I don't know. I've only really slow danced."

"This is New Orleans," he coaxed. "It's time to learn how to party."

Without giving her breathing room, he pulled her out onto the dance floor. He had learned that giving Trinity too much time to think left her paralyzed. Sometimes you had to jump-start the action to get her to, well, act.

She shouldn't have worried about her dancing. They shared lots of laughter, lots of teasing, and some very sexual tension. Finally, the band slowed enough that he could pull her close, and bury his fingers in the curls now falling at the nape of her neck.

It wasn't until he glanced sideways and caught sight of Patricia and Richard watching from the wings that he remembered exactly why he was on the dance floor. According to their smug expressions, it was time to start worrying.

# Thirteen

"I just think it would be an interesting way to include donors in the everyday running of the charity," Trinity concluded as she set her plate on the breakfast table the next morning.

Heavy clouds loomed outside, warning of an incoming thunderstorm. It still felt like early morning, even though they'd skipped their customary breakfast in favor of an early lunch. Rhett had been grateful for the extra time to sleep. They'd gotten in late after dropping a very chatty Madison off at her home. After the sleepless hours Rhett had spent trying to brainstorm a way out of this whole mess, he was grateful they were getting a late start on their day.

Feeling sluggish, he simply wanted to stretch out on one of the chaises beneath the bougainvillea vine and soak in some warmth. The weather had other ideas. Also, Trinity was firing on way more cylinders than he was this morning.

"Don't you think?" she asked.

He grunted as he lifted his first cup of hot, black chicory coffee to his lips.

She shot him a half grin. "Rough night?"

"You have no idea."

He thought she whispered, "Oh, I probably do," but he couldn't be sure.

He'd wrestled half the night with his decision to put Trinity on display at the party last night. Even though she hadn't felt it, he had known what he was doing. His body was tense with anticipation for the call letting them know a new post was up. It would come today.

At least these photos were something he could control, rather than something the Hyatts cooked up on a whim to damage Trinity's reputation further.

Their phones buzzed almost simultaneously. Rhett didn't bother to look at his. His focus was on Trinity.

He watched as she checked her notifications and turned pale. The guilt washed over him, forcing him to squeeze his eyes shut for a second, maybe two. Then he heard the clatter of her phone on the table and her footsteps as she ran back into the house.

By the time he opened his eyes, she was gone.

He wanted to run after her, but knew he needed to see what had been posted. Her reaction had been unusually strong.

Reaching across the table, he picked up her phone. The screen lit up as he turned it to face him. Rhett blinked for a moment, his brain not quite comprehending the image. The video still showed the face of a man he didn't recognize. It wasn't until he scrolled down to the headline that it all made sense.

### Widow's Father Confirms She is
### After Money

*Nice.* Guess he wouldn't be winning any father-of-the-year awards, now would he? But the man never had before, so why start now?

At least Rhett knew what Patricia had been scheming.

He walked with heavy steps up the stairs to Trinity's room. Somehow he knew she would be there, surrounded by her books and artwork. He almost expected her to be curled up in the bed. Instead, he found her braced, her back turned as she stared out the panoramic windows.

Even from this angle, he could tell she had her arms locked around her stomach. Was she crying? Was she raging? Whatever she was doing, it was too quiet for Rhett's comfort.

"Trinity, are you okay?" he asked, wincing even as he said the words. Of course, she wasn't okay. That was a stupid question to ask. But where else could he possibly start?

"I'm fine," she said, her tone biting and cold.

"It's all right to be upset."

"Oh, I'm not upset." The tremor in her deadly quiet

voice set off alarm bells. As she turned to face him, he saw no evidence of tears.

"I'm not upset," she repeated. "I'm furious. How dare he? How dare they?" She stomped across the open space, then turned and headed back again.

Rhett felt like he'd sold his soul for nothing, even though he knew this wasn't about him. He had no clue how to make this right. At all. But he had to find a way. He wanted to hold her, comfort her in a way he'd never thought he was capable of, but the emotions bouncing off of her kept him at bay.

So he let her pace it out, hoping his continued presence, his willingness to listen was enough.

"You know what makes me angry?" she asked, her voice loud enough to ring in his ears. But he refused to wince as she went on. "I'm not angry for myself, but for my mother."

She paced back to the window, laying her palm against the glass as if to feel the water running down the other side. "You see, I know whatever he says, he's lying. He always has. I'm old enough to remember." She released a soul-deep sigh. "I remember his lies, to us and to himself."

She shook her head. "My mother never contradicted him, never argued. Maybe she put up with his abuse longer than she should have, but she tried to keep peace in our house." Her hand dropped to her side. "Until she knew she couldn't anymore." She turned to face him. "It's a losing battle when you're up against someone stronger than you."

She absently rubbed her fingertips over the scar

above her right ear. "She made the choice to leave, but the lies didn't stop until someone more powerful stepped in. Only Michael was able to truly gut him from our lives. My father just wanted control. He would have plagued us forever without Michael's help."

She pointed a shaky finger toward her phone in Rhett's hand and he reflexively squeezed it. "Whatever he said about us, it's a lie. But my mother isn't here to defend herself, is she?" The way she hugged herself made his chest ache. "Would she want me to? In the midst of all the other chaos in my life, do I really want to engage with…this? Counter whatever he might have said about us? Or ignore it all?"

She slumped forward. "It's all so exhausting."

Rhett bent forward until he could meet her gaze with his own, his chest aching at the emotion in her brown eyes, and asked, "Does he even deserve a response?"

She shook her head adamantly. "No, he doesn't."

"Then we'll let Bill deal with it," he assured her. "Whatever he said."

He approached her with cautious steps, for once unsure exactly how to comfort her. "You aren't alone in this," he said. "It may feel like it sometimes, but you aren't alone." The twinge of unease as the words left his mouth was muted. Over the past few days, he'd become more comfortable being there for her. He wasn't sure how it had happened. If it was simply the sheer peace of her presence, the purity of her drive to do the best for everyone involved, or the draw of her sophisticated beauty…but the change was definite.

To his surprise, he welcomed it.

He didn't know what the next action to take was or how to fix any of this. But the peace was there. The conviction that she didn't deserve any of what the Hyatts were doing to her.

The belief that Michael had made the right choice.

Then Trinity took a deep breath, looked down at her phone still in his possession, and asked, "Will you watch it with me?"

If Trinity had ever thought she'd see her father again, it had never occurred to her it would be in a rainy room in Michael's house, in full color on the screen of her phone with Rhett's arm securely around her.

She took a deep breath against the sense of unreality as the video began to play.

Her father's face was more bloated than she remembered. Probably from years of drinking the beer he'd always liked so much. At least he appeared tidy and clean-shaven. But she could still recognize the essence of his character in the features. What he truly was.

A bully.

"I was never nothin' but good to 'em." To Trinity, the slight whine in his voice set her on edge. "Until they fell in with that Hyatt dude. I wasn't wanted for nothin' after that."

The interviewer's voice was disguised, sounding mechanical as he or she asked questions from off-screen. "Where did they meet Michael Hyatt?"

"Don't rightly remember," her father replied with a shrug. "They was always disappearing, not telling me where they'd go."

Trinity could feel herself tightening up, barely able to contain the rebuttals running through her head. Her inner defenses were hardening. She forced herself to remain silent, as if to prove something to a man who wasn't even in the room.

Her father continued, "Guess all that money and a fancy house was too much to turn away from."

The interviewer asked, "So your wife wanted money?"

"Doesn't every woman?"

Rhett coughed, then cleared his throat. He hugged her a little closer.

Her father continued, "Nothin' I did was ever good enough for 'em. They was always whining and crying. Enough to put me in a rage."

Guess the audience wouldn't realize quite how accurate his words were.

"I'm pretty sure if that girl of mine was in the right place, she'd take full advantage of getting in that guy's pants—"

"Oh, turn it off," she snapped.

Rhett paused the video and stared for a long moment at the frozen screen. "How awful," he muttered.

Trinity turned her head to look up at him, watching his throat muscles work as he swallowed.

He pulled back a little so he could look down at her. The slight frown between his brows touched her. Very few people would care about her feelings in this matter. Life had taught her that much.

"How are you?" he asked.

A sad sort of chuckle escaped, surprising her. "Actually, it's a relief."

"Why?" he asked, the frown digging a little deeper.

"Because that man is obviously full of himself. My memories were right."

Rhett nodded slowly. "But not everyone will see that. Even if they do…"

"That's not my problem."

Trinity struggled to put her sudden apathy into words. It wasn't really that she didn't care. Some part of her did. But the overwhelming feeling at the moment was a kind of numbness seeping over her, giving her a respite from the constant upset caused by other people's actions.

She'd been *reacting* since she'd first learned of Michael's death, and faced public outrage over the inheritance. Even before that, going back to when Michael had asked her to marry him and told her the reason for his request. It was as if her own emotions were being played by an orchestra of other players, but she never got to voice her own personal song. The numbness was a relief on several levels, even though she sensed it was a protective move to shut down the roller coaster she couldn't seem to get off.

"These past weeks have taught me the hard way that I can't control what everyone thinks," she said. "The reality doesn't make me happy—I've spent my life trying to help others—but it's foolish to sit around and stew about it."

Still, the struggle wore her down. Why, for a few minutes, could she not be happy? She wanted to actually live rather than simply struggle to breathe. To figure out the fix to everything around her.

She glanced down, her gaze catching on the sight of Rhett's hand on his thigh. So strong. So masculine. She remembered the feel of it on her body, and wished for once that she hadn't chickened out the other night.

Maybe there wouldn't be any repercussions. At her age, maybe he wouldn't even be able to tell that she'd never been with anyone else. After all, who would suspect it? She inched her fingers over to his, then let them glide over his skin in a tiny stroke that felt awfully big.

Lightning flashed outside the windows, followed moments later by thunder loud enough to shake the house. The storm was raging. Wind beat against the house with the full ferocity of nature. It mirrored Trinity's emotions.

She swallowed the lump of fear in her throat and wrapped trembling fingers around Rhett's palm. She could sense his gaze on her, but couldn't force herself to look up.

She wanted this for herself, this one thing. And she would have it.

"Trinity?"

A questioning, searching tone, but not a rejection. She took a moment to gather what little courage she could find, then forced herself to look up and meet his gaze with an open one of her own.

She could see when the realization hit him. Of their own accord, her fingers stroked over his hand again. She allowed herself to test the textures of his skin. To ground herself in the moment and let the last weeks of turmoil completely slip away.

The last time he'd touched her, he'd been hesitant, almost as if he were asking for permission. This time, he already had it. With firm confidence, his hand slid up from her shoulder into the fall of her hair. The feel of him cupping the back of her head made her want to melt into his warmth. Her neck, shoulders and back relaxed in automatic response.

Her eyelids slid down. In the darkness, she could focus on the touch, smell and feel of him. The rain against the windows and roof created a cocoon where it was only the two of them. The rest of the world washed away beneath the deluge.

He twisted his upper body toward her. He began massaging her scalp with both hands. Breathy moans escaped her parted lips, but she couldn't stop them. Refused to smother them. They blended with the ping of raindrops.

Then his lips covered hers.

Giving herself over to her desires, Trinity refused to hold anything back. She reached out, grasping the front of his shirt with her fists. Her head spun with the overwhelming sensations. Being able to just feel, instead of constantly thinking, left her desperate for more.

No one had ever done this for her...except Rhett.

Then suddenly he was gone. Trinity opened her eyes to find him standing beside the bed, his gaze darkened with an intensity that made her shiver. His body shadowing her made her feel small but not afraid. Rhett had never used his strength against her; he never would.

But now he crowded forward. She crawled back. Their gazes remained locked.

As she reached the middle of the bed, he grabbed her foot with both hands. She watched as his skillful fingers found each buckle, loosened each strap and slid each foot free. Since when had removing sandals been so sexy?

Then, one at a time, he enveloped each arch in his big hands and began to work magic. Squeezing, rubbing, pressing… Trinity let herself fall back onto the comforter, no longer able to hold herself upright as her body rejoiced. The focus wasn't just on her feet; every inch of her seemed to revel in his expertise.

Then he guided her feet until they rested flat against the top of the bed. Her legs were spread wide beneath her flowing skirt, knees bent. She knew it wouldn't be any barrier at all. He loosened his tie, pulling it off over his head. Then he unbuttoned the first button on his dress shirt. Then the next. Then the next.

Finally he paused, fingers poised to finish the job, and asked, "Are you ready?"

# Fourteen

$R$hett blew out a heavy breath, attempting to steady his fingers. The shaking was unexpected. Of the intense emotions buffeting him right now, nervousness wasn't one of them.

He refused to think about what that might mean.

Instead, he focused on stripping down to his boxers quickly so he could turn his attention where it mattered. To Trinity.

Her reactions seemed just as intense as his. Gratifying, for sure. But more important, they fed his own response in a way he'd never experienced before. It was a mutual exchange of energy that pushed them both higher. He wanted to experience every part of Trinity with a thirst that went beyond mere physical desire...and he wanted the same for her.

Rhett slipped his hands beneath her skirt to cup the backs of her knees. Her skin was soft, silky smooth. He swallowed hard on a moan. Palms flat, he traced her supple muscles up to her hips, feeling as if he'd been granted something very special, something only between the two of them. When his fingertips found the edge of her panties, he paused, letting another breath out. Her hips lifted slightly, granting permission. He could hear her panting, see the desire in her eyes even as the thunderstorm darkened the room further.

Hooking the fabric in his thumbs, Rhett pulled her panties down. He watched their slow progress beneath her skirt, down her legs, his body throbbing its approval. Somehow knowing she was naked yet still clothed blew the top off what seemed so simple. So sexy.

Her naked toes dug into the duvet. He wanted to touch them again, kiss them. But urgency pushed him higher.

Just as he had done with his own shirt, he unbuttoned hers one button at a time. Her pale skin peeked out between the parting fabric. Ribs and stomach trembled with her rapid breathing. He peeled back the layers, groaning at the sight of her breasts encased in pale pink lace. Trinity was a lady down to her skin. But her watchful gaze told him he held the key to turning this proper lady into the woman she ached to be.

He buried his face in the smooth skin of her stomach, taking in her sweet smell accented with a hint of need. She pressed against her heels, raising her body to meet him. He traced her contours with his lips, then nestled his face between her breasts. He let his body ease down onto her, testing her tolerance for his weight. There were no protests, only clutching hands and tilting hips.

She felt incredible beneath him. Her tiny gasps told of her aching need, ratcheting his own higher and higher. Her fingers dug into his back, urging him to give her more.

He tried to hold out, tried to make himself wait so he could indulge in this experience as long as possible. He popped open the front clasp of her bra, then swept one cup aside to free the trembling mound beneath. Her skin was so pale he was almost afraid of leaving marks. But he couldn't stop himself from touching her. He followed her lead, learning what made her gasp, what made her moan and what made her beg.

Only when he couldn't ignore the urgent pull of his own body did he finally slip his hand beneath the flimsy barrier of her skirt once more. Lying on his side next to her, he could watch her face as he found her most precious of spots. Knowing he might not be able to control himself later, he forced himself to lock down his desires and focus on hers. With exquisite expertise and a dawning wonder, he teased her body.

Her expressions of surprise and excitement fascinated him. He could have gotten drunk off the headiness of pleasuring her. Her cries echoed the thunder. When he could hold himself back no longer, he pressed his fingers urgently against her. The firm lift of her hips and her silent scream only fed his own pleasure as he slid his fingers firmly inside of her.

He didn't expect the resistance, the tightness, the

way her pleasure turned to a gasp of pain. He immediately froze.

She didn't move, so he tried again. This time, she let out a cry of discomfort.

"Trinity?"

He wasn't prepared for her to squeeze her thighs together, to force him out. She shook her head. "I didn't realize…" she moaned. "I've never…"

*Virgin.* The word echoed through his brain. That couldn't be right. There was no way—

*Virgin.* Rhett pulled back, from her, from the bed… How was this possible? He'd done his due diligence. He'd asked the common questions about her marriage. He'd watched her, spied on her, seen how they'd lived. Nothing too unusual for the rich types he'd spent his life watching. Nothing to indicate…this.

*Virgin.* She hadn't been intimate with Michael as his wife. Their marriage hadn't been normal…real. Did that mean the Hyatts were right, in a way? Had she somehow duped Michael into an arrangement that gave her access to his fortune…but no intimacy in return? What had she been to Michael, if they hadn't fully consummated the marriage?

Memories of being duped into what would have been a similar relationship flooded his mind. The hurt. The betrayal. Had Michael known before he married Trinity? Had she tricked him into marriage, then reneged on the deal later?

Rhett suddenly realized that he was now standing beside the bed, staring down at Trinity. His heart raced. No desire remained, only a growing wave of betrayal.

The realization that Trinity hadn't told him the real truth. How had he let this happen to him *again*?

With that thought echoing in his brain, he met Trinity's look with his own and said, "How could you keep this from me? Let me think that..." He ran a harsh hand through his hair. "Let me think your marriage was real. That your relationship with Michael was real."

He ignored the frantic shake of her head, the way she sat up and wrapped her shirt tightly over her nakedness. Instead he let that sense of betrayal build, connecting with the remnants from that confrontation with his fiancée so long ago. He'd told himself he would never be vulnerable to a woman again. Yet here he was.

Now another woman had drawn him in with her sweetness and charm, feeding him the bits and pieces she wanted him to see to gain his help and favor with the Hyatt Heights board. He thought back to his ex-fiancée, how she'd been gaming him for his fortune. He'd narrowly escaped her scheming but it had left a permanent scar.

Rhett had spent the rest of his adult life making sure other people didn't get scammed like he had. Like his father had. Now look at him.

The first woman to make him question the convictions built by years in this job had proven that she wasn't what she seemed. She wasn't a devoted, grieving widow in the true sense. She could very well be someone who'd scammed Michael out of his fortune.

It was the first time Rhett had ever turned his back on those instincts. He'd believed Trinity wasn't capable of deceiving him, wouldn't even want to. And yet, here they were.

A flash of heat swept over his skin—a mixture of anger and embarrassment. He wanted answers, but couldn't even formulate the questions. He paced back and forth, needing an outlet for the emotions ricocheting inside of him. Finally, he halted next to the window, pivoting to stare at the woman still sitting on the bed.

Her expression had smoothed to a blank mask, just as he'd seen it do in times past. But this time, he wondered what she was hiding beneath the smooth façade. Trinity just sat like a blank doll in the middle of the bed.

Silent.

Deep inside, the urgent need to know the truth she'd been hiding from him spread. He didn't care how dark or ugly her secrets were. He needed to know the scope of the deception that had broken every last instinct he'd relied on to guide him for years. He had believed in her and she'd let him down.

"Tell me the truth. The real truth," Rhett demanded from across the room, running a rough hand through that silver-streaked hair.

Trinity had felt a slight relief as he'd moved away from her. Common sense told her she had nothing to fear from him. At least, physically. But then again, she'd never seen him under this amount of pressure, expressing this much emotion. And life had made her cautious.

Her vocal chords remained frozen. She should have accepted the inevitable and kept Rhett firmly at arm's length. But she hadn't. She'd been greedy, wanting something for herself.

And ended up in this nightmare.

There was no going back. But how could she explain the truth she'd been living? Rhett saw her marriage as a lie. Michael had seen it as security. For Trinity…it had been the only way to say thank you to the man who had saved her life.

"I should have trusted my instincts," Rhett said as he paced across the room. "People said you were a gold digger. How could I have just brushed that aside? Your marriage *was* a lie. I want to know just how much of one."

In an instant, the deep freeze inside Trinity melted. Gathering a cloak of stoicism around her, she eased herself to the edge of the bed and rearranged her skirt over her legs. To the best of her ability, she blocked out Rhett's critical presence across the room. With steady effort she put her bra back on, then buttoned up her shirt.

Only when she'd finished did she realize he'd stopped speaking, stopped pacing.

She turned her gaze in his direction, thankful for the shadowy room and the sense of protection it gave her. She doubted she could have handled this conversation in a spotlight of sunshine.

"What do you want to know?" she asked.

Her voice wasn't as steady as she would have liked, but at least she wasn't going to break down crying. Showing weakness never led to anything good.

His voice was low, but gravelly with emotions. "Why are you a virgin?"

"Because I've never had sex, of course."

She couldn't interpret what his grunt meant. That she was telling him something obvious? Couldn't they just skip to the part where this conversation was over and they both knew where they stood? That would be great. Yeah...

"You were married to Michael."

She nodded, not trusting her voice. The next question was a given.

"So why are you a virgin?"

"Because Michael wasn't able to consummate our marriage."

Rhett's deep intake of breath told her he was going to demand more answers, so she plunged forward, hoping not to have to break her final promise to Michael. "Even if he'd been able to, Michael would not have wanted to have sex with me. I told you, and everyone else who would listen... Michael was my best friend. We were friends since I was a kid. But he was not romantically interested in me."

"Then why on earth would he marry you?"

Trinity buried the sting of those words deep down inside.

"Michael wanted to protect his estate from his aunt and uncle. He knew their interests in his assets stemmed from their desire to sell them off. The only way to keep that from happening was to have another heir."

"It's not the only way...he could have simply willed it to you."

"Which he was doing. But Michael wasn't taking any chances. He knew they would challenge whatever he put in place. The more ties he could create, the better chance his choice would be honored in court."

"So he planned to what? Use you as a surrogate?" His incredulous tone wreaked havoc on her nerves. "Have children but not sex?"

This time she couldn't hold back a wince. It was never nice to know that someone thought you were good enough to be used, but not worthy of the true experience of love.

"I never said that."

Not that Michael had meant it that way. But Trinity had known that by doing as he asked, she was giving up on her own dream of a family in her own way. Not that prospects had been beating down the door of *Maison de Jardin* to date her. Yet another reason why she was having this conversation...

She tried to distract him instead. "We didn't share a room. You knew that."

"Lots of couples do that. But they still have sex. Especially on their honeymoon. You were married a week, for Christ's sake. Hell, you'd known each other a whole lot longer. Why wouldn't he—"

The urgency in his voice told her his frustration was growing. How long could she hold the questions at bay? Was it a betrayal of her dead husband if she told the truth? The whole truth?

His next question was delivered with very tight control. "*Why* did you marry him?"

Trinity pressed her feet together, wishing she had

shoes on. Then she pressed her knees together, and her thighs. The precise movements distracted her from her acute distress. "Because he asked me to."

"This wasn't a simple marriage, a *normal* marriage."

"No," she finally conceded. "Michael had very specific demands for our marriage. It was my job to fulfill them, whether he was here or not."

"*Job*. So this *was* a business arrangement? I should have known."

*More of a legacy.*

She tilted her head back to meet his gaze. That direct confrontation was hard for her, but she knew better than to avert her gaze. That would just make her look even more guilty.

"So he paid you?" he persisted.

She could feel her mind pulling away, shrinking away from the implications of his words.

But Rhett wasn't backing down. "Did he pay you to pretend to be his wife?"

"Not in the way you think," she answered, hating how small her voice sounded next to his.

Only then did she notice the coolness streaking down her cheeks. Tears. Trinity wasn't sure when they'd started, only that they were gathering along the curve of her jaw and falling to her shirt below. She refused to reach up and brush them away. That would only highlight their existence.

"Enlighten me," Rhett said. "I refuse to be fooled again. Not in this lifetime. Not by you."

Just like that, her heart cracked. Weariness seeped out to spread through her body and flood her system. It was all she could do to keep herself upright. She'd spent her life supporting others. It was her purpose, her calling. First her mother, the women at the shelter, Michael.

For one glorious moment, she'd thought she'd found someone who could be there *for her*, *with her*, in Rhett. Now she knew that wasn't going to happen. Not the way she wanted.

After this, he'd never feel the same way about her again.

So why continue to fight the inevitable? Weariness weighed her down. Maybe if she told him the truth, he'd leave her to grieve in peace.

"Michael needed a wife very quickly."

"And he chose you?"

"He knew he could trust me."

Rhett shook his head, denying the truth. "Why would a man in his position trust you? Why would he let himself get into a situation where he had to?"

"There are things in life even the rich can't control." Still her loyalty refused to give in, to unlock the words held inside for so long.

"Such as?"

It took some effort to force the forbidden words past the tightness in her throat. "Michael was very sick."

Rhett froze. "How sick?"

Trinity squeezed her eyes closed, then broke her promise to her best friend. "Stage four pancreatic cancer."

# Fifteen

Rhett heard the words but felt them more like a blow. The knowledge that Michael had been that sick, facing his own mortality, could support either interpretation of Trinity's motives...depending on which side he wanted to take.

"There were no remains left to test," he said.

Trinity shook her head. At least the tears seemed to have stopped for the moment. He hadn't liked how the sight of them softened him.

"No," she said. "Dying in the helicopter crash meant no true evidence of his illness except protected medical records. No way to prove he was dying already. No way to judge the severity of his illness. And no way for the Hyatts to claim he wasn't in his right mind when he chose to marry me to protect his charity. Unless the judge could get the medical records released...if he even knew to ask."

"Was he?"

Trinity glanced up at him, her expression resigned. "Was he what?"

She knew what he meant, but she was going to force him to state the obvious, huh? "Was he in his right mind?"

"Right until the last minute. I was on the phone with him just minutes after the helicopter took off. Though luckily not when they went down. According to the investigation, the accident was a mechanical malfunction...not deliberate tampering."

Despite his roiling emotions, Rhett was glad Trinity hadn't been on the line to hear it as it happened. It was something he wouldn't wish on his worst enemy.

"Michael knew exactly what Richard and Patricia would do with his estate once they had their hands on it. His doctor had only given him a month, at best. He wanted everything in place before he announced our marriage."

Her shaky breath brought on a mixture of guilt and skepticism Rhett still couldn't quite suppress.

"I promised Michael I would protect his secrets and protect his vision for the future of the charity. He knew the board would help me run the companies, though he'd hoped to make his own announcement about me taking his place...closer to time."

"So why open up about this at all?" Rhett didn't like the hoarseness of his voice, the hint that he might be buying a tale he couldn't corroborate with the man himself. His demands would not have made her tell him this sacred of a truth if she'd been determined to keep the secret from him.

For just a brief moment, a grief so visceral flashed through her stoic expression that Rhett actually took a step back. But that didn't protect him from her words.

"You're the only person who has seen every part of me. What's the point of holding back anymore?"

In that moment, Rhett knew that words would never have convinced him. Neither would papers or files or signatures. That one flash of emotion proved to him that Trinity was on the level.

And that he was a total asshole.

Simply because experience—the very thing that had warned him not to trust her—had taught him that emotions that intense could not be faked. There was always a hint of insincerity. Something Rhett was a master at sniffing out. But with Trinity, there had been nothing to hold that grief back...and to know that he had caused at least part of it meant he was lower than low.

Rhett usually trusted his instincts. The fact that he'd been warring with them the whole time he'd been with Trinity had worn him down. But this time, he would listen without hesitation.

He crossed the last few steps to her side, noting for the first time how he'd pressured her. Oh, on some level, he'd surely known that, but only now did he acknowledge it.

So when he reached her, he knelt down, forcing himself to look up at her instead.

"Trinity, I only have one more question," he said.

She tilted her chin back to meet his look, mask once more in place, even though every line in her body spoke of a weariness he knew had to go bone deep. "Yes?" she asked.

"Will you forgive me?"

She shook her head as if to clear it. "I don't understand."

Rhett felt awkward and juvenile and humbled. He'd made assumptions based on his past and hers that he shouldn't have. Why should he expect her to understand? He wasn't sure how he'd make it right but he refused to let himself skate through this.

"I told you, once before, that I'd been betrayed. By a woman."

She nodded, the blank mask she'd adopted softening with curiosity. Seeing that genuine emotion told him he was on the right track.

"Well." His throat tightened as he grew more reluctant to give up his secrets. But it was only fair, as much as he had refused to discuss this in the past. Only two other people knew: his partner and his father. But after what he'd said to her, she deserved an explanation rather than living with the belief that this was all her fault.

"My ex-fiancée… I found out quite by accident that she'd decided to marry me not for love."

Trinity remembered his earlier words about his ex-fiancée and her quest for riches. "Oh, Rhett. I'm sorry."

He shrugged, though his feelings on the matter were far from casual. That one incident had changed the course of his entire life. "I'm sure there are any number of men who would have been happy with that arrangement if they'd have known about it up front. I was not comfortable, nor happy. She had targeted me and come into the relationship knowing that's all she wanted, but spent months convincing me her feelings were much, much deeper. So I broke our engagement in quite a cold fashion."

"What happened to her?"

"She went on to marry a man within our social circle… twenty years her senior."

Trinity gave off an air of growing awareness, as she seemed to grasp the similarities between the situations. "I see."

"He was a retired military man. Quite well-off. Once she became pregnant, I simply couldn't handle even chance meetings. I embraced my—work—and was grateful to be away on travel more often than not."

He'd wished that their encounters hadn't bothered him, that he'd felt nothing at all. Instead every time he'd seen her, the barbs had sunk deeper. Which in turn fueled his passion for his work. Though he'd never accused anyone of going after money without proof, he had to wonder now if he'd missed something along the way.

He certainly had with Trinity. Or rather, he'd lost his own ability to sniff out the truth.

"It's not an excuse. Rather, an explanation." Hopefully one that would help her feel better when the time came for her to know the whole truth.

In this moment, he realized he wasn't going to be able to hide who he really was from Trinity. She deserved better. And for this to move forward—whether just toward healing or an actual relationship—he would have to be honest. Only he didn't know how to do that yet.

He glanced back at her, only to find her gaze brushing hastily over his chest. Because it was bare? Did that part of him, any part of him, still attract her?

Heat pooled low in his belly, urging him to return to the sweetness of their first encounter.

Her first encounter.

His heartbeat sped up. He shouldn't. But he wanted to. Then her gaze lifted to his and he saw the spark there also. She still wanted him. But was he doing the right thing? Or the selfish thing? Could he walk away and let Trinity feel rejected by yet another person in her life who should care for her?

For the first time in this whole situation, Rhett led with instincts alone. "I lied. I actually have one more question."

"What's that?" Trinity asked, caution drawing out the two words. He didn't blame her. But he could show her another way.

"Will you let me stay with you?"

Trinity called herself every kind of fool for even entertaining the idea. But her body remembered. Her body wanted. She'd never thought she'd be the type of person who could give her body without letting her heart be fully involved, but for just once in her life, she considered risking the heartache to have this one moment with him. Could she wall off her heart for a little while so she could have this memory of him?

A moment she might never have again.

She tried to let reason prevail, just as she had her entire life. "I'm not really sure that's a good idea," she said, though she didn't even sound convincing to herself. It *wasn't* a good idea. Things between them were already messy and complicated. He was probably doing this out of guilt.

"I know, and that's my fault," he said, confirming her thoughts. "I want to make it up to you."

Her body went cold at his words. She didn't want someone who felt like he *had* to be with her. But he had wanted her earlier. She might be innocent, but she wasn't naive. Rhett had wanted her.

Could he want her again?

Out of the corner of her eye, she looked him over once more. His button-down shirt hung open, leaving his sculpted chest and abs in partial view. Her mouth watered. Remembering the feel of him against her didn't help keep her on the straight and narrow.

Half-dressed and his hair askew from running his fingers through it, Rhett was the sexiest man alive. In this moment, there was only one thing that would keep her from indulging.

She forced her chin up once more, took a deep breath and plunged ahead. "I don't want this to be about me." She swallowed hard, forcing the words out despite her churning emotions. "I would want it to be about us."

It took a minute for her meaning to hit him, but she could see a visible change when it did. His body relaxed for a moment, then every inch of him tightened. Those gorgeous gray eyes and wide smile lit up the darkened room. He looked like she'd given him a gift.

The last thing she wanted was for this to be about making up for his judgments. That wasn't how she wanted to remember it. Because she knew without a doubt that soon a memory would be all she had.

Suddenly the air in the room changed, as if it had been electrified. Rhett reached out a hand to her. She wasn't sure what he had in mind. A moment of panic contracted her lungs. But she couldn't stop herself from reaching out, from taking what she truly wanted.

Tears burned against her eyes as he helped her to stand facing him. She would do this and keep those emotions tucked deep inside. There was no way for her to eradicate them. She'd always been emotional. But she'd had a lifetime to perfect how to hide them. She only hoped that skill served her well today.

Rhett rubbed the back of his knuckles right beneath her jawbone, then tucked his hand down along her neck. The feel of him against her sensitive skin made her shiver. His fingers slowly worked her top buttons open.

Her reaction this time was just as aroused as before, only mixed with anxiety over what was to come. She mourned the loss of that pure excitement, but willed away the sadness with each brush of his knuckles against her skin.

Once all of the buttons were undone, he slipped the shirt back and off her shoulders, leaving her in her skirt and bra. She expected him to go straight for that front clasp. Instead he traced her shoulders with his palms, then trailed them down her arms to her hands, igniting all of the nerves along the way.

After a moment, he lifted her hands to the opening of his shirt.

Startled, she glanced up. He watched her through a hooded gaze that sent her temperature soaring upward, but he gave no verbal directions. She grasped each lapel and squeezed tight. Could she do this?

The citrusy smell of him mixed with the smell of fresh-fallen rain from outside. The scent filled her head. She tightened her grip. There was no way she could give up on this, even though there was no future in it for her. There couldn't be.

But she blocked that out and focused only on the moment. On slipping her hands beneath the panels of his shirt. On the smooth texture of his skin stretched across taut muscles, except where a sprinkling of hair broke the heated expanse. Trinity let her eyes close, concentrating on the feel of him beneath her palms. She brushed her fingers along the edge of his waistband, then down the front of the cotton boxers.

How she had the courage to cup the hardness of him, she wasn't sure. His groan echoed in the air. It was a music her entire body was attuned to. She wasn't sure if she would melt or tense when he touched her, but she was very sure the heaviness growing low in her belly was all for him.

When he put his hands on her, all hesitation ended.

A trail of fire traveled over her skin, led by the touch of his hands, then his arms, his chest, then there wasn't a single part of them that didn't touch. Bare skin pressed against bare skin was more intoxicating than she'd ever imagined it could be. And when he laid her down on the bed, his muscled body covering hers, she thought she'd found heaven.

There was barely a hint of pain this time, just an unfamiliarity as his body stretched hers. She lifted her hips, eager to be wholly a part of their coming together. Not passive or accepting. She couldn't keep her hands still. Instead, they pulled him closer, tracing the muscles of his arms and back as he worked over her body.

The feel of him moving with her, her minute responses to his every movement, left her breathless. He buried his mouth against her throat. Every nerve ending in her body went electric. She heard herself cry out. Her nails dug into his back.

As his own cries filled her senses, she knew she'd just created the memory of a lifetime.

# Sixteen

"Son, only you could find yourself in this situation. I've always told you this line of work would come back to bite you."

It was so easy to picture his father on the other end of the phone, with his head full of silver hair, seated in his favorite armchair before the fire in Seattle dispensing those words. Rhett would have grinned at the fond indulgence in his father's voice, if he wasn't in some serious need.

"I chose this line of work, as you call it, because I wanted to help people."

"You mean help expose people? People like your ex-fiancée, and your stepmother, and—"

"Dad," Rhett interrupted in a warning tone.

"It's a legitimate question. You don't need to work.

So why would you do this day in and day out? Why would you do something that just keeps you mired in suspicion and lies?"

*Because I'm good at it.* Or rather…he had been.

"Well, this would definitely be the moment you've been predicting for years," Rhett conceded, but he wasn't ready to give in completely. "But I would like to point out that I've never been wrong before."

"There's always a first."

"This is a pretty unique first," Rhett said, his brain distracted with thoughts of the woman he'd left working in the office at Hyatt House and the unusual challenge he'd found in her.

"I'd say," his father agreed. The story had just come tumbling out as soon as Rhett had found a safe space, and a safe ear, to talk.

"I just…" He hated to admit this, but he didn't see that he had any choice. He couldn't see where to go from here. His usual strategic plans had failed him. "I know Trinity is hardworking and doing her best to take care of both the charity and the employees of the companies. I've seen it in her dedicated study and brainstorming and conscientious work. I have no doubt I could win her case in an instant if I testified to everything I've seen. But—"

"But?"

"You and I both know that her being a virgin would be a damaging piece of information in a court case over her dead husband's inheritance." *Tell me I'm making the right choice. Was he looking the other way because he wanted to be right? Because he wanted Trinity to be innocent?* "At the very least, once the public got ahold of that information, it could be used to sway the board against her."

"It could."

He let the silence play out for a minute, not wanting to ask the question outright. But he finally gave in and said, "Am I missing something?"

"You've seen evidence of her true character with your own eyes?" his father asked, no-nonsense and able to zero in on the essence of the problem just as Rhett had known he would.

"I have."

Rhett thought back over the past few weeks, trying to look beyond the looming memory of last night. He knew he was being swayed by the intensity of becoming Trinity's lover…her first lover. "I believe her to be a good person. A person who's trying to do what's right by the charity and the businesses." Unlike the Hyatts.

"Then trust those instincts."

"But—" Hell, he couldn't actually love her… Could he?

"Trust them. I'm learning to."

*What?* "Dad, what have you done?" Slight panic sliced through him as he wondered what his father had gotten into while he'd been halfway across the country.

"I've found Candy."

"Really, Dad? A woman named Candy?" He shouldn't be biased against a name, but considering his father's choices in the past…

"Yes, sir. And my instincts are leading me true."

He'd be the judge of that. Taking care of his father had always been his job. "I'll decide that when I get home. Do not sign anything."

"No, you won't. And I don't need to. She has her own money."

That's what they all wanted them to think. "Dad—" There was no one else to step in. He had to protect his dad's heart from being crushed yet again.

"Rhett, it's time for you to let go."

There was no force in his father's voice. No harsh directive. Only a calm acceptance that Rhett couldn't quite grasp.

"What are you talking about?"

"Son, despite our family's history of unfortunate encounters, there is still happiness to be had in this world. I'm ready to have it, rather than holding it at arm's length because I'm afraid."

"I'm not afraid."

"I beg to differ. Otherwise, why would you be calling me for an opinion? You're a strong, decisive young man. You don't need me to tell you what to do. Your instincts will lead you."

They hadn't been helping so far. Rhett felt like this whole case had been one challenge to his instincts after another.

"Now, as for this young lady of yours... She'll be tried in the court of public opinion, regardless of what the judicial system says."

He'd known his father would get it right off. "Exactly." And Rhett did not want to watch her go through that. But how did he warn her without coming clean about himself?

He would do whatever he could to prevent the Hyatts from getting the information he now knew. But what about the rest? "I don't know how to protect her."

"You can't."

"But knowing what she'll face alone…"

"You can't stop the reality from coming to her." His father sighed. "We both know that. When she chose to help her friend, like you said, she chose what she would face. You can only stand beside her. Guide her. Uplift her. But you can't protect her."

But he wanted to. For the first time in his life, he wanted to protect someone from the consequences of her actions, rather than expose them. Thinking about the soft, sensual woman he'd held last night being vulnerable to Richard and Patricia Hyatt as he'd come to know them turned on a fierceness Rhett didn't know how to handle. And knowing that he'd been part of the plot to destroy her made him feel ashamed.

"I don't want her to find out about me."

"You know it will never stay a secret."

"I do know that." The question was, would he lose her over it? He deserved to, but that didn't keep him from wanting to fight to keep her.

Trinity frowned at Rhett as he sat at the small table across the room from her desk. He wasn't working. Instead he stared out the window at the sunshine that had finally decided to make an appearance.

She didn't care that he was slacking off. It was the

infernal tapping of the pen he held against the papers in his other hand. *Tap. Tap. Tap.* Whatever he was thinking so hard about had him oblivious to the noise that Trinity couldn't ignore.

"Are you okay?" she finally asked, her voice a little louder than she intended in the quiet office.

With a start, Rhett glanced her way. "Yes. Why?"

She dropped her gaze to the pen, which he'd stopped tapping. "Just wondering."

He didn't acknowledge her look, but she knew he got her point because he gripped the pen in his fist. Still he didn't say a word. So as much as she didn't care for confrontation...

"Plus, you've been acting weird all day." She cleared her throat, not sure where she got the courage to say the rest. Why did adult relationships come with so many difficult conversations? "You know, if you regret yesterday, it's okay. I won't hold you to any implied commitment."

His raised brows indicated a surprise almost as big as hers for having said anything in the first place. Then a smile spread across his sculpted lips, offering a hint of relief to her growing angst. "No, Trinity. It's nothing like that."

"But it is something, right?"

*Busted.* She almost laughed at the consternation in his face and the way his body tightened up. If there was one thing she was good at in her life, it was reading people. Rhett wasn't hiding the signs very well.

Before she could tease him, the door to her office swung inward.

Of all the people she'd expected, Patricia and Richard were not the ones. She tensed.

Jenny rushed in after them. "I'm sorry."

"Leave us," Patricia demanded.

If she hadn't been so nervous, Trinity would have laughed at the way Jenny held ramrod straight, refusing to leave until she received the nod from Trinity. Some people still understood loyalty, and Trinity was grateful for the few people in her life that hadn't turned their backs on her since Michael had passed.

"What can we do for you, Patricia?" she asked as the door closed with a quiet snick.

"Rhett, so nice of you to join us," the other woman said instead of answering.

Rhett stood, bracing himself as he faced the Hyatts. "I didn't realize I'd been given a choice." The Hyatts exchanged a glance that he ignored. "As Trinity asked, what can we do for you?"

Richard chimed in this time. "Oh, it isn't about what you can do for us. We have an offer you won't want to refuse."

Patricia glanced Trinity's way with a smirk. "Especially you, my dear."

"What?" Trinity did not like where this was going. The very vibe of the room had changed, darkening despite the sunshine streaming through the slats of the blinds.

Add the fact that Patricia and Richard never visited Hyatt House outside of business meetings, and this felt wrong on every level.

*An ambush.* Trinity's stomach tightened, bracing herself against the wave of malevolence in Patricia's look.

"We are here with a very sweet offer for you, my dear," she said, her smarmy tone contrasting her steely look.

"Then talk to her lawyer," Rhett broke in.

Richard raised a brow, confusing Trinity as he said, "Careful now."

Rhett clenched his teeth, his face freezing even as his gaze was shooting daggers into the other man. The level of emotion between the two men seemed out of proportion, though Trinity appreciated Rhett's defense.

She frowned, further unsettled. "Look, if this is about the court case, Rhett is right. You need to speak to Bill."

"I don't think it will go to court. *Now.*"

"Why?" Trinity braced herself for yet another blow. After all, that's what the Hyatts were good at, right? But she could hope... "Are you withdrawing your suit?"

"No, but you will withdraw your objections and willingly turn the estate over to us."

Trinity huffed out her surprise, glancing around at the other people in the room. "Um, no. I won't."

Patricia stalked closer. "Of course, you will. Unless you want us to reveal everything we know about you to the court."

"And what would that be? I have nothing to hide. And someone has already made my past an open book on social media, so—"

"Oh, I'm sure the judge will be very interested to learn that you were a virgin when your husband died.

Non-consummation might have some influence over how he decides the case."

Trinity felt her body go ice-cold down to her finger-tips. Even her brain froze, keeping her from uttering a single protest. Then a sickening wave of heat washed over her. She swayed before steadying herself. If there was one thing she would control in this meeting, it was whether or not she would go down.

Rhett stepped into the outer edges of her vision. "Non-consummation does not change whether or not she can receive his inheritance. The judge won't be influenced by that."

"But public opinion might," Richard said. "I'm sure the board would love to be led by a woman accused of enticing a lifelong friend into marrying him, then not even gifting him with her body before stealing his money."

"Stop it," Trinity barked, struggling for air but unable to hold the words back. "That has never been true."

"The public doesn't care." Patricia smirked before she went on. "And I'm sure a certain Instagrammer will be happy to spread the news for us…as well as how we found out that juicy little tidbit."

In that moment, Trinity realized her first mistake was that she hadn't denied their claim immediately. Second, in her shock, she hadn't even thought about how they'd found out about it. There were only two people who knew. Her…and…

She turned her gaze to Rhett, who stood still as a statue without a single denial on his lips.

"Please tell me you did not do this," she pleaded, ashamed that the words had to pass her lips.

"I did not," he said, not averting his gaze from the snakes in their midst.

"Oh, he pretty much did, though he didn't include it in his weekly report."

Trinity blinked. "I don't understand."

"Oh, you will," Patricia said, her tone indicating just how much she relished delivering the blows to her enemy.

Richard jumped to fill in the details. "Your boyfriend here has been working for us the whole time."

"As a business consultant? Larry brought him in."

"No." Patricia's smile was wide and satisfied. "As a spy."

Trinity's throat went dry. She licked her lips, wondering where all the moisture in the room had gone.

"He was brought in to tell us everything we needed to know about you to break your claim on Michael's estate. And he has."

Rhett stalked forward. "I don't know how you got that information, but it was not from me. And I told you just now that is not a legally binding reason for her not to inherit."

Patricia didn't seem to care. "You will withdraw your claim and sign everything over to us, free and clear. Otherwise, we will discuss your sexual history, or lack of it, in court, for it to become public record."

She glanced at Rhett. "If you're lucky, we will keep silent about your part in this. Not make your little career public news."

"You signed a nondisclosure agreement," Rhett said, squashing Trinity's last bit of hope that this was all a nightmarish mistake.

Patricia turned to leave before throwing her final words over her shoulder. "You have seventy-two hours to comply."

# Seventeen

For the first time in a long time, Rhett had no words. Maybe for the first time in his lifetime.

As he watched Trinity stare into her room from the hallway later that day, he knew they had to talk this out. But she looked so forlorn as she watched an army of staff pack her belongings, he knew he couldn't put it off for long.

He still didn't understand why she wanted to move out. The first thing she had done upon leaving the office downstairs—without a word—had been to instruct Jenny to have her stuff packed and a moving van called.

With an excess of caution, he stepped up beside her and asked, "Why are you doing this? It's crazy."

Trinity was silent for so long that he wondered if she would answer at all. Finally she said, "You know,

I've long known that there were advantages to having money. But when you have none, it's hard to imagine them in detail. The possibilities don't occur to you, because they would never be an option under normal circumstances. That's why people consider the behavior of celebrities eccentric. Only now I realize, if I want to move in a matter of hours, as opposed to days or weeks, I can."

She tilted her head just enough for him to get a glimpse of her profile. Of her strained smile.

"And no one can stop me," she said.

"You don't have to do this. Don't give in to them, Trinity." Of all the things happening right now, he did not want Trinity to lose this incredible space Michael had created for her.

For a moment, her tone went from flat to hard. "Do you really think I'd ever want to sleep in that bed again? Ever?"

And that was all on him.

He didn't know who had overheard him talking, but someone had to have passed that information along to the Hyatts. Now that he thought about it, maybe getting her out of this house was for the best. The last thing she needed was someone spying on her...someone *else* spying on her.

*Damn.*

"I promise you I did not tell them—"

She cut him off. "I do not care to speak about that."

Should he honor her wishes? Should he push this?

"Will you go to *Maison de Jardin*?" He wasn't even

sure why he asked. After all, it wasn't like she had another family home to return to.

"Yes. For now."

A safe house. Exactly what she needed right now. He wished he could be with her, but he would need time to figure all of this out.

"You're welcome to stay here as long as your contract with the Hyatts permits," she said. "But I'm not paying a dime past yesterday for your consulting services to Hyatt Heights."

"I understand—"

"I doubt you do. But I'm being more than generous. My only stipulation is that you stay the hell away from me."

Rhett searched hard for something to say, feeling her slip away with every word. "Trinity, I didn't know you when I took this job."

"Is that really your job?" She cocked her head but still refused to look him in the eye. The sphinxlike profile that had intrigued him from the beginning was set off nicely by the warm wood doorframe behind her. He took in the high cheekbones. Thick eyelashes. Delicate nose. Her fragile beauty made his shame even worse.

"You've made a career out of discrediting people?"

He wasn't surprised by the sheer disbelief in her tone. She'd thought she'd known him. Now she faced the reality of his lies. He'd never worried about the people he left behind before this. Of course, many of them didn't know he'd exposed their dishonesty. He didn't stick around for that part.

The reality of his chosen career wasn't pleasant or

comfortable. Watching Trinity have to suffer for it made it feel like someone was tearing tiny little wounds into his heart every few minutes.

"I simply gather information about people and pass it along to the clients who need to know it." Even he could tell he was grasping for an explanation. He'd never been ashamed of what he'd done until this morning. But looking at it through her eyes...

"You spy on people," she clarified for him. "I thought you were helping me, teaching me." The words choked off for a moment.

*Loving me.* He'd refused to acknowledge it, but now he could see what had been happening all along. Rhett had risked his heart—something he'd vowed not to do for the last ten years. Now here he was, trying to figure out a way to fix the situation that he'd complicated with his own lies.

Still, he was grateful to see at least a glimpse of emotion. The last thing he wanted for Trinity was for her to be permanently locked behind the blank mask caused by her wounds. She should not have to live like that.

"I'm sorry," he said, then had to clear his throat as the emotions constricted it. "I've been trying to find a way to get you out of this for a while." And he still would, somehow.

"Why bother?"

Reaching out, he used his knuckle to guide her chin in his direction. He waited until her brown eyes met his before he said, "I expose people who deserve it. People who are trying to steal from others. It didn't take me long to realize that you weren't one of those people."

Her eyes widened slightly, exposing the whites, before she turned away once again. His fingers went cold immediately. Her voice was once again distant as she said, "It doesn't matter now. Once they realize I'm not giving in, the Hyatts will make sure no one believes anything I say anyway."

No. No. No. "It doesn't have to be that way. We can ask Bill to make it inadmissible in court." Anything to keep her from being further exposed to the judgment and condemnation she'd already experienced.

"In court or on the internet…what difference does it make?"

The hopelessness in her tone seeped under his skin. "Then don't do it. Walk away."

"Why? So y'all can win?"

"No." He dragged one of his hands through his hair, wishing he could pull it out by the roots. "Because fighting for this in court is not worth your reputation, your sanity, Trinity."

She shook her head slowly, sadly. "Have you ever owed someone your life, Rhett?"

He swallowed hard. "No."

"Then you wouldn't know if it's worth it or not." She started to walk away from him down the hall. "Right now, I simply want to be back in the only home I've ever really known. For as long as I'm allowed to be there."

Rhett returned to his own room, unable to handle the sight of her walking away from him. He deserved it. He knew that. But he wasn't ready to give up yet. Pulling out his cell phone, he dialed Larry's number.

"Tell me you have something for me. Now."

\* \* \*

"I can't believe I'm one of those women who is fussing over what to wear," Madison said, then let out an exasperated sigh. "Living in a sickroom means dressing for comfort and flexibility. Not in frills and ruffles."

Trinity gave her a half-hearted smile. "I don't really think you're the ruffles type."

"Definitely not." Madison shuddered. After accepting a date with the man she'd met at the fund-raiser, her nervous preparations had begun. "But I figure a man like him will be expecting more than jeans and a T-shirt."

"You never know. Everyone has their own preferences."

And their own secrets. That had never hit home for Trinity more than it had over the last three days. With her deadline for the Hyatts fast approaching, her thoughts were consumed with worry and need.

Any minute now, her secrets would be spilled to the world. She just wasn't sure which direction they would come from. When she wasn't talking herself out of a panic attack over it, she was wondering what had happened to Rhett. She shouldn't care, shouldn't want to know. Yet she found herself obsessing over whether he'd gone back home—wherever that was. And whether he'd given the Hyatts more details about their encounter. Whether he cared about the humiliation she was about to face.

She shouldn't spare him a single thought. So why was he all she could think about?

Madison got up as the kettle on the stove started to

sing. The house was relatively quiet at this time of the day, with the children in school or day care, and most of the women at work or in classes. Madison had come by to check on Trinity and immediately set about making tea when she saw how listless she was. Trinity wasn't used to having so little to do. Her days had always been full to the brim with charity stuff, then after Michael's death, it had been the business. Being at loose ends was not boding well for her sanity.

Madison's chatter about her upcoming date was a welcome distraction.

"I don't even know what we're doing. It's a surprise," Madison said as she set up the tea and poured. "Do you think we'll have anything in common?" She cupped her hands around her teacup as if to warm them. "I'm used to spending time alone, a lot. I hope he doesn't find that weird."

"You'll be fine," Trinity assured her. Her brain raced with warnings she wanted to pass on to the younger woman, but she kept her mouth shut because she knew they were a product of her current situation.

"I'm sorry," Madison said.

Trinity looked up from stirring her tea. "Why?"

"I'm prattling on about some guy. That's probably the last thing you're interested in right now." She offered a small smile. "I just don't really know what to say to make any of the things you've experienced better."

"Don't be sorry. It actually helps take my mind off things."

Any minute, the other shoe would drop. She'd instructed Bill that she would continue to deny the Hyatts' control of Michael's estate. She had no doubt now that they would drive it into the ground, starting with *Maison de Jardin*. Regardless of whatever paperwork had been signed between the other parties, Trinity was not bound by any nondisclosure agreements. She would do whatever she had to in order to defend the estate from Michael's greedy relatives.

After all, people's livelihoods and protection were more important than a little humiliation on her part. But so far, news had been quiet.

Too quiet.

"I just can't believe Rhett was working with those people." Madison shook her head. Trinity had shared some of the bare bones of the situation once she'd moved back to *Maison de Jardin*. "He seemed genuinely interested in the charity while he was here. Surprised by everything we did to help these women get back on their feet. I thought he was a good guy."

"Me, too," Trinity said softly. "Guess we can be taken in by just about anyone, huh?"

"Scary."

"I see women come through here all the time. Their husbands or boyfriends are charmers at the start. Until they become controlling, petty, angry. Then they change." Because it was all about them, never about the women they loved.

"Did Rhett change?"

"Yes, but I thought it was for the better. Now I know it was just another lie."

Madison squirmed in her chair, reminding Trinity that she was speaking to someone on the verge of a new relationship. She shouldn't be ruining it for her. Despite everything, Trinity wanted to believe love was possible…just for other people. Not for her.

She'd never risk her heart…or her body…again.

"It will be okay, Madison."

The younger woman smiled, but Trinity couldn't miss the knowledge in her eyes. Madison might not have been abused, like many of the women in this house, but her life had never been an easy one. That was for sure. She deserved some hope.

"You go and have a good time, Madison. Everything here will work itself out. I promise."

As if to challenge her words, her cell phone started to ring. Trinity hesitated when she saw Bill's name. It took a moment of gathering what tatters of grace she had left before she could answer.

"Yes?"

"Have you seen the new blog post?"

"No, Bill," she snapped. "It's not like I have alerts set up or something." She'd finally turned them off. She was tired of knowing about it the instant bad news made its way out into the world.

"You might want to take a look at this one. I'll call you in a little while."

Trinity rolled her eyes as she ended the call. She'd thought women were melodramatic. They had nothing on silver-haired Southern lawyers. She stared at her phone for long moments, unable to force herself to open the internet browser. Her mother had taught her to face life head-on. Trinity was fast losing that lesson these days.

Maybe she could hide in her cave for another five or six hours?

The doorbell rang, providing a welcome distraction. As she and Madison headed for the front foyer, the weight of her phone in her hand reminded her of everything she was avoiding. Had they gone to the gossip blogger with stories of her virginity? How she'd duped Michael out of his inheritance? Why was no one willing to believe that she'd done all of this to help a friend?

She needed to stop hiding and at least arm herself with the knowledge of what she would be facing over the next few weeks. Pausing on the edge of the foyer, Trinity forced herself to unlock her phone.

Just as she clicked on the app, Madison opened the front door. Trinity couldn't look up from her search. Now that she'd determined what needed to be done, she had to do it immediately. She didn't hear the steps approaching her. Instead, when the blog opened on her phone, she scrolled down to the first picture and was shocked to see Rhett Brannon.

Then his voice intruded, "Hello, Trinity."

Looking up, she found herself staring into those gray eyes in person.

# Eighteen

**R**hett followed Trinity into the sitting room attached to her bedroom at *Maison de Jardin* and slid the door closed behind him. He wasn't taking any chances on anyone overhearing them. What he had to say was too important, too personal.

When she reached the slim side table near the window, literally as far from him as she could get, she stopped and turned to face him. "If you've come to talk to me about the blogger, save your breath. I see you've done some kind of interview…just like my father."

He wouldn't admit to anyone how much it hurt to be lumped into the same category as her abuser. "Have you watched it?"

"Not yet."

Well, he had been impatient to see her again. Maybe

he should have waited another hour or two, but he hadn't been able to stay away. Her closed expression and short answers weren't giving him much hope.

"Do you plan to?"

"Why? What will I hear? A first person account of how I threw myself at you to lose my virginity? That would make for really sensational gossip, wouldn't it?"

A spark of frustration lit inside him. "I would never do that to you."

"I don't know you at all," she argued. "How would I know what you're capable of?"

How could he prove he was trustworthy? He'd done the only thing he'd known to do. Now he needed her to watch it.

"I've always been me, Trinity. Yes, I hid things about myself, especially in the beginning. But I strive to give as much of the truth as possible."

"So you don't slip up?"

He couldn't really refute it. That's exactly why he'd done it in the past. "Given the nature of my job, what do you want me to say to that?"

"I honestly don't know."

He did. She was angry and lashing out, and she had every reason to. He should be soft and accepting but that wasn't Rhett. If there was a playbook for winning back the woman you loved after being a complete horse's ass, he hadn't read it. But he wasn't about to let her shut him out with anger.

"I'm not going to apologize for doing my job, but I am sorry for how it ended up hurting you." He took a deep breath. "Now let's move on to something more productive."

Oh, she didn't like that. Her body tensed and she wrapped her arms around her stomach. "Okay, then answer some questions for me," she demanded. "How in the world do you make a living doing this?"

Wow…from shaky ground to even shakier. "Since I don't need the money, it's not really a true living."

"You do this for *fun*?"

From her tone, her anger was growing. "No. I do it to keep people like me from being taken advantage of. From being lied to and stolen from."

That softened her just a little. At least, her voice. "Your fiancée?"

"It happened to me. It happened to my father. People lie and steal all the time."

She thought about that a moment. "So you run a sort of undercover security company."

"Not anymore."

She shook her head. "What?"

"First, no one is gonna hire me once they watch that." He gestured to her phone. Her eyes widened as the implications started to take hold. "And second, I don't think I have the stomach for it anymore." He couldn't take his eyes off of her, even though she refused to look at him directly. "A sweet Southern woman taught me a better way."

She shook her head, squeezing her eyes closed. "I can't. I can't do this, Rhett."

"Yes. You can." He stepped closer. "I know you've

been hurt. I know *I* hurt you. But I'm trying to fix this, to make it right."

"By spilling even more of my secrets?" The fear and sadness in her eyes made his stomach churn. "Did you tell them about Michael? About how sick he was? That was a confidence I gave you. I promised him I wouldn't tell—"

"I didn't." Rhett grabbed her shoulders and gently shook her. "I promise I did not tell them anything you wouldn't want me to." He wanted nothing more than to end the panic and pain on her face. "Watch it," he said. "Now." He needed her to see.

Rhett cringed as his voice on the recording filled the room, but he refused to move away from Trinity. He would be here with her through this, even if she didn't want him, until he knew she was safe. Safe from the Hyatts and safe from him.

Even though he couldn't see the screen, Rhett recognized the tinny distortion of the interviewer's disguised voice asking, "Can you introduce yourself, please?"

"I'm Rhett Brannon, currently contracted as a business consultant for Hyatt Heights, Inc."

"So you were requested to help Trinity Hyatt learn to run the businesses she stands to inherit from her late husband, is that correct?"

"Through Hyatt Heights, yes."

"Are you employed by anyone else?" the interviewer asked.

"I'm not at liberty to say."

"Are you contractually obligated to deny answering that question?"

Rhett hesitated before he answered. "Yes. I've signed a nondisclosure agreement with another entity who required me to work closely with Trinity Hyatt. Something she was unaware of at the time."

"Since we are very concerned here about whether this woman is qualified to carry on Michael Hyatt's enterprises, can you tell us whether you believe she duped her dead husband into giving her his businesses?"

Rhett remembered how this part of the interview had made his blood pressure rise, though he couldn't hear any anger in his response. It had probably shown on his face, though.

"I've interacted extensively with Trinity Hyatt, with her lawyer and the staff at Hyatt House who knew Michael Hyatt after years of working with him. There was no duplicity on her part. She and Michael were very close friends for many years, and I believe that's the reason he asked her to marry him."

He paused a moment before going on. "People get married for many different reasons. We assume, in this day and age, that it's either for love or for money. But that's not always the case. I believe Michael saw in Trinity someone who could complement him in business, in social situations and in companionship. That was his choice to make. Unfortunately, he passed away before he could make the world understand why he made that choice."

Rhett went on to talk about his experience with Trinity in business matters. He'd kept it as general as possible, to avoid any legal trouble for himself or Trinity. He and Bill had briefed the blogger on what he could say, which hadn't stopped the person from asking him, "If Trinity Hyatt is such a good person, why do you think so many bad things have come out about her?"

Rhett remembered the punch of sadness that had accompanied his answer. Trinity had never deserved the things dished out to her since Michael's death.

"Two things. First, money talks. Greedy people will say whatever they want to get people on their side. Especially if saying those things profits them in some way. We can't change that, only counterbalance it as best we can. In the end, people will believe what they want. Second, drama sells. There's a reason why controversy is what you end up posting about on your blog and social media channels. Because more people will click on it, read it. We don't need more drama in our lives."

He took a deep breath before he went on. "We need love. Trinity taught me that."

Rhett tensed, recognizing the moment the interviewer went off script.

"I've heard a rumor that Michael and Trinity Hyatt's marriage wasn't consummated. Can you confirm that for us?"

Trinity abruptly paused the recording. "I can't. I just can't hear this," she said.

He laid his hand over hers, aching as he felt the slight tremor beneath his palm. "Trust me, Trinity," he said. "Trust me to do right by you."

She didn't, he knew that. He deserved it. But she didn't deserve to live without faith. Doing this interview had been just as much about giving that back to her as setting the record straight. "Please."

It took a few seconds. But like the strong woman he knew, she finally pushed the button so she could listen.

On the video, Rhett said, "I've heard that rumor, too, and it makes me sad."

"How so?" the interviewer asked.

"Michael Hyatt was a trusted member of this community, held in high esteem by his fellow members of society, the members of his board and by his employees. Why can we not trust his judgment? He chose Trinity. For whatever reason, he chose her. Why do we not believe he knew exactly what he was doing when he made that choice?"

"People get duped all the time," the interviewer insisted.

"Not by people they've known for over fifteen years," Rhett said, his own experiences with Trinity bolstering his confidence. "He knew Trinity since she was a child. He knew what he was doing. Trust that."

Trinity gave a small squeak, but he didn't turn to look at her, afraid of what he would see.

"Do you think the Hyatts will win?" the interviewer asked.

Rhett thought for a moment before he responded, "They'll continue to fight. And because they are willing to fight dirty, they might even win. I've offered to testify as much as I can on her behalf. But all Trinity can do is her best. For Michael's sake, for the trust he put in her, I know she will give it her all."

Rhett listened as the video wound down, hoping his words were enough to make Trinity see how he believed in her. He may not have been able to win the case for her, but he hoped he'd been able to make the path an easier one.

Trinity couldn't stop the shaking deep down in her core. The fact that Rhett had protected her privacy meant the most to her, but he'd also defended her...and defended Michael.

"Why are you doing this?" she asked, barely able to force her voice above a whisper.

"I want to make things right," he said, but the way he fidgeted while they watched the video, his tense stance and clenched fists, indicated it wasn't as simple as that.

"Why?" she pushed.

Something was missing. She needed to know more.

Whatever was missing was big. Trinity could tell as Rhett pivoted on his heel and stalked to the far side of the room. His hands dug into his hair, making it stick up at odd angles. Oh, yeah, this was big.

Was she ready?

Finally, he blurted out, "There's something I left out."

Was she ready? Did she really want to know? Trinity swallowed hard, then asked, "What?"

To her surprise, Rhett connected his gaze to hers. There was nowhere for her to hide from the emotion in those gray eyes. "That I love you," he said with a quiet intensity that shook her foundation.

She could only blink. "Why?"

He gave a huff of laughter. "Trinity, so often you sell yourself short. You're intelligent, intense, hardworking, compassionate." He strode back over to her, as if he couldn't stand to be that far away from her. It felt good…though she didn't want to admit it. "And you're beautiful in every way. Even if I lose you through my own sheer stupidity, I will never, ever be able to forget you."

Each word hit her heart like a knock on a door, begging her to open and let him in. Did she dare risk it? What if—no. No more questions. She would have to step out in faith, like her mother had always told her.

"Why didn't you tell them that on the video?" she asked.

"Because not everything should be public."

*Good answer.*

"I can't stop what the Hyatts may put out there about you. And I'm horrified about the part I played in giving them that information."

"How did it happen?" Trinity needed to hear him say it for herself.

"Someone spying on the spy." His mouth twisted in a sarcastic smile. "I believe someone overheard me having a conversation over the phone about conscience with my father…when I thought I was alone."

"With your father, huh? About me?"

Rhett nodded. "For the record, he's never approved of my career choice, despite some episodes in his life inspiring it. Our family isn't the luckiest in love."

Rhett hesitantly reached for her hand as if to underscore his words. He brushed his fingertips along the back first, then slid them around to completely envelop her hand. Ever so slowly, she curled her fingers up around his. Accepting, but still cautious. His smile said he understood.

Okay, she wasn't going to even think about him telling his father she was a virgin. It was too embarrassing, even though she could now understand the issues it raised for him.

"Well, I found myself in a unique situation," Rhett said, "and he was eager to make me admit I wasn't always right about these things."

"Smart man." Trinity smiled at the idea of his father trying to keep Rhett humble.

"We've had some ugly times, he and I. He's never agreed with how I've handled it."

"Betrayal by someone you love is never easy," she murmured. "I'm sorry you both had to go through that."

"I'm not. I wouldn't be here if we hadn't. If I hadn't."

"I know the feeling."

"I wish you didn't," he said, taking her face between his palms. "I've done so many things wrong since I've met you, but I want the chance to make it right.

"Which reminds me," he said, "I've investigated a few things through my connections, and my suggestion to you is to get rid of Maggie. She's head of the daytime housekeeping crew, by the way, and has contacted Patricia Hyatt on her cell phone several times."

Trinity remembered the slight woman, though she'd rarely had much to do with her. Had that been on purpose?

She couldn't stop herself from reaching up and cupping his cheek. She didn't want to talk about them anymore, to give more headspace to the people who had set out to harm her. "What about the things you've done right?"

"They're hard to remember when I see the pain on your face."

"Let's try," she said, wishing she could erase the regret from his expression. "You believed in me, encouraged me, protected me in a room full of gossips eager for blood."

"They were quite rabid."

"So I think, all in all——" she paused to swallow "——you might be a keeper."

"Are you sure? An unemployed thirtysomething with a father to take care of and a sad track record with relationships. I think *I'm* the risk now."

"Are you sure about giving up your company for me?"

Rhett pulled her close, speaking against her hair. "My father told me it was time to let go. I've decided he was right."

"I learned something from my father, too."

He squeezed her a little closer, the comfort of having his body against hers something she couldn't believe she was actually experiencing.

"What's that?" he asked.

"I learned that some people's actions can make you angry or sad or amused or irritated. But there is only one reason that someone's actions truly hurt."

"Why, Trinity?" he whispered against her.

She knew he regretted what he'd done. It was there in his touch, in his tone. As much as she hated to hurt him, she needed him to understand this.

"It only hurts if you love them."

That had him drawing back, looking deep into her eyes with that incredible gray gaze. "Thank you, Trinity. Nothing could ever mean more to me than knowing you love me."

"I do." The words truly were a vow, though they weren't standing in a church to say them. She'd never loved another man like this. Though putting her trust in him was scary, her heart compelled her to forge ahead.

Reaching out with shaking hands, she cupped Rhett's face and pulled him down until his lips touched hers. "I'll never leave you to face life alone again," he promised. "I'll always be beside you."

As his hands traveled over her body once more, she reveled in his touch. Only Rhett had ever made her feel this incredibly electric, as if her nerve endings were attuned solely to him. Somehow, like her mother had said, there'd been a man made just for her. And he'd come to make her mind and heart and body sing.

Without any fanfare, Rhett joined their bodies together. It couldn't have felt more right. The solid support of the table beneath her. The firm presence of his body between her thighs. The way he paused, fully inside of her, as if to savor this moment with her.

"I love you, Trinity," he said low as he pressed their bodies as close as possible. "I always will."

Together. Forever.

\* \* \* \* \*

*If you loved this story
of passion and betrayal,
don't miss Madison's story!*

Reclaiming His Legacy
*by Dani Wade*

*Available March 2020
from Harlequin Desire.*

# WE HOPE YOU ENJOYED THIS BOOK!

Experience sensual stories of juicy drama and intense chemistry cast in the world of the American elite.

Discover six new books every month, available wherever books are sold!

Harlequin.com

# AVAILABLE THIS MONTH FROM
## Harlequin® Desire

## FROM BOARDROOM TO BEDROOM
*Texas Cattleman's Club: Inheritance* • by Jules Bennett

Sophie Blackwood needs the truth to take back what rightfully belongs to her family. Working for media CEO Nigel Townshend is the way to do it. What she doesn't expect is their undeniable attraction. Will her feelings for her British playboy boss derail everything?

## BLAME IT ON THE BILLIONAIRE
*Blackout Billionaires* • by Naima Simone

Nadia Jordan certainly didn't plan on spending the night with Grayson Chandler during the blackout, but the bigger surprise comes when he introduces her as his fake fiancée to avoid his family's matchmaking! But even a fake relationship can't hide their real chemistry...

## RULE BREAKER
*Dynasties: Mesa Falls* • by Joanne Rock

Despite his bad-boy persona, Mesa Falls ranch owner Weston Rivera takes his job very seriously—a point he makes clear to meddlesome financial investigator April Stephens. Stranded together by a storm, their attraction is searing, but can it withstand their differences once the snow clears?

## ONE LITTLE INDISCRETION
*Murphy International* • by Joss Wood

After their night of passion, auction house CEO Carrick Murphy and art detective Sadie Slade aren't looking for anything more. But when she learns she's pregnant, they must overcome their troubled pasts for a chance at lasting happiness...

## HIS FORBIDDEN KISS
*Kiss and Tell* • by Jessica Lemmon

Heiress Taylor Thompson never imagined her night would end with kissing a mysterious stranger—let alone her reluctant date's older brother, Royce Knox! Their spark can't be denied, but will family and professional pressure keep them to just one kiss?

## TEMPORARY WIFE TEMPTATION
*The Heirs of Hansol* • by Jayci Lee

To keep his role as CEO, Garrett Song needs to find a bride, and fast. And Natalie Sobol is the perfect candidate. But their marriage of convenience is rocked when real passion takes over. Can a bargain that was only supposed to be temporary last forever?

---

**LOOK FOR THESE AND OTHER HARLEQUIN® DESIRE BOOKS
WHEREVER BOOKS ARE SOLD, INCLUDING MOST BOOKSTORES,
SUPERMARKETS, DISCOUNT STORES AND DRUGSTORES.**

HDATMBPA0120

### #2713 FROM BOARDROOM TO BEDROOM
*Texas Cattleman's Club: Inheritance* • by Jules Bennett
Sophie Blackwood needs the truth to take back what rightfully belongs to her family. Working for media CEO Nigel Townshend is the way to do it. What she doesn't expect is their undeniable attraction. Will her feelings for her British playboy boss derail everything?

### #2714 BLAME IT ON THE BILLIONAIRE
*Blackout Billionaires* • by Naima Simone
Nadia Jordan certainly didn't plan on spending the night with Grayson Chandler during the blackout, but the bigger surprise comes when he introduces her as his fake fiancée to avoid his family's matchmaking! But even a fake relationship can't hide their real chemistry...

### #2715 RULE BREAKER
*Dynasties: Mesa Falls* • by Joanne Rock
Despite his bad-boy persona, Mesa Falls ranch owner Weston Rivera takes his job very seriously—a point he makes clear to meddlesome financial investigator April Stephens. Stranded together by a storm, their attraction is searing, but can it withstand their differences once the snow clears?

### #2716 ONE LITTLE INDISCRETION
*Murphy International* • by Joss Wood
After their night of passion, auction house CEO Carrick Murphy and art detective Sadie Slade aren't looking for anything more. But when she learns she's pregnant, they must overcome their troubled pasts for a chance at lasting happiness...

### #2717 HIS FORBIDDEN KISS
*Kiss and Tell* • by Jessica Lemmon
Heiress Taylor Thompson never imagined her night would end with kissing a mysterious stranger—let alone her reluctant date's older brother, Royce Knox! Their spark can't be denied, but will family and professional pressure keep them to just one kiss?

### #2718 TEMPORARY WIFE TEMPTATION
*The Heirs of Hansol* • by Jayci Lee
To keep his role as CEO, Garrett Song needs to find a bride, and fast. And Natalie Sobol is the perfect candidate. But their marriage of convenience is rocked when real passion takes over. Can a bargain that was only supposed to be temporary last forever?

"Do we know each other?"

Her sharp but low intake of breath glanced off his ears, and he faced her again, openly scrutinizing her face for any telltale signs of deception. But she was good. Aside from that gasp, her expression remained shuttered. Either she had nothing to hide or she was damn good at lying.

He couldn't decide which one to believe.

"No," she whispered. "We don't know each other."

Truth rang in her voice, and the vise squeezing his chest loosened a fraction of an inch.

"And I guess I didn't see the point of exchanging names. If not for this blackout or you being in this hallway instead of the ballroom, our paths wouldn't have crossed. And when the power is restored, we'll become strangers again. Getting to know each other will pass the time, but it's not because we truly want to. It's not...honest."

Her explanation struck him like a punch. It echoed throughout his body, vibrating through skin and bone. Honest. What did he know about that?

In the world he moved in, deception was everywhere—from the social niceties of "It's so good to see you" to the cagey plans to land a business deal. He wasn't used to her brand of frankness, and so he didn't give her platitudes. Her honesty deserved more than that.

"You're right," he said. "And you're wrong." Deliberately, he straightened his legs until they sprawled out in front him, using that moment to force himself to give her the truth. "If not for me needing to get out of that ballroom and bumping into you here, we wouldn't have met. You would be outside, unprotected in the parking lot or on the road. And I would be trapped in the dark with people I wish I didn't know, most likely going out of my mind. So for that alone, I'm glad we did connect. Because, Nadia…" He surrendered to the need that had been riding him since looking down into her upturned face and clasped a lock of her hair, twisting it around his finger. "Nadia, I would rather be out here with you, a complete stranger I've met by serendipity, than surrounded by the familiar strangers I've known for years in that ballroom."

She stared at him, her pretty lips slightly parted, eyes widened in surprise.

"Another thing you're correct and incorrect about. True, when the lights come back on and we leave here, we probably won't see each other again. But in this moment, there's nothing I want more than to discover more about Nadia with the gorgeous mouth and the unholy curves."

Maybe he shouldn't have pushed it with the comments about her mouth and body, but if they were being truthful, then he refused to hide how attractive he found her. Attractive, hell. Such an anemic description for his hunger to explore every inch of her and be able to write a road map later.

Her lashes fluttered before lowering, hiding her eyes. In her lap, her elegant fingers twisted. He released the strands of her hair and checked the impulse to tip her chin up and order her to look at him.

"Why did you need to escape the ballroom?" she asked softly.

He didn't immediately reply, instead waiting until her gaze rose to meet his.

Only then did he whisper, "To find you."

*Find out what happens next in*
Blame It on the Billionaire
*by* USA TODAY *bestselling author Naima Simone.*

*Available February 2020 wherever*
*Harlequin® Desire books and ebooks are sold.*

Harlequin.com

# Get 4 FREE REWARDS!

## We'll send you 2 FREE Books plus 2 FREE Mystery Gifts.

**Harlequin® Desire** books feature heroes who have it all: wealth, status, incredible good looks... everything but the right woman.

**FREE** Value Over **$20**

---

**YES!** Please send me 2 FREE Harlequin® Desire novels and my 2 FREE gifts (gifts are worth about $10 retail). After receiving them, if I don't wish to receive any more books, I can return the shipping statement marked "cancel." If I don't cancel, I will receive 6 brand-new novels every month and be billed just $4.55 per book in the U.S. or $5.24 per book in Canada. That's a savings of at least 13% off the cover price! It's quite a bargain! Shipping and handling is just 50¢ per book in the U.S. and $1.25 per book in Canada.* I understand that accepting the 2 free books and gifts places me under no obligation to buy anything. I can always return a shipment and cancel at any time. The free books and gifts are mine to keep no matter what I decide.

225/326 HDN GNND

Name (please print)

Address                                                                 Apt. #

City                            State/Province                    Zip/Postal Code

> **Mail to the Reader Service:**
> **IN U.S.A.:** P.O. Box 1341, Buffalo, NY 14240-8531
> **IN CANADA:** P.O. Box 603, Fort Erie, Ontario L2A 5X3

Want to try 2 free books from another series? Call 1-800-873-8635 or visit www.ReaderService.com.

---

*Terms and prices subject to change without notice. Prices do not include sales taxes, which will be charged (if applicable) based on your state or country of residence. Canadian residents will be charged applicable taxes. Offer not valid in Quebec. This offer is limited to one order per household. Books received may not be as shown. Not valid for current subscribers to Harlequin Desire books. All orders subject to approval. Credit or debit balances in a customer's account(s) may be offset by any other outstanding balance owed by or to the customer. Please allow 4 to 6 weeks for delivery. Offer available while quantities last.

**Your Privacy**—The Reader Service is committed to protecting your privacy. Our Privacy Policy is available online at www.ReaderService.com or upon request from the Reader Service. We make a portion of our mailing list available to reputable third parties that offer products we believe may interest you. If you prefer that we not exchange your name with third parties, or if you wish to clarify or modify your communication preferences, please visit us at www.ReaderService.com/consumerschoice or write to us at Reader Service Preference Service, P.O. Box 9062, Buffalo, NY 14240-9062. Include your complete name and address.

HD20

# *Love Harlequin romance?*

## DISCOVER.

Be the first to find out about promotions,
news and exclusive content!

Facebook.com/HarlequinBooks

Twitter.com/HarlequinBooks

Instagram.com/HarlequinBooks

Pinterest.com/HarlequinBooks

ReaderService.com

## EXPLORE.

Sign up for the Harlequin e-newsletter and
download a free book from any series at
**TryHarlequin.com.**

## CONNECT.

Join our Harlequin community to share
your thoughts and connect with other
romance readers!
**Facebook.com/groups/HarlequinConnection**

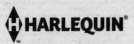

**ROMANCE WHEN
YOU NEED IT**

HSOCIAL2018